Elliot

and the Last Underworld War

JENNIFER A. NIELSEN
ILLUSTRATED BY GIDEON KENDALL

sourcebooks
jabberwocky

Published by Sourcebooks Jabberwocky, an imprint of Sourcebooks, Inc.
P.O. Box 4410, Naperville, Illinois 60567-4410
(630) 961-3900
Fax: (630) 961-2168
www.jabberwockykids.com

Library of Congress Cataloging-in-Publication data is on file with the publisher.

Source of Production: Bang Printing, Brainerd, Minnesota, USA
Date of Production: March 2012
Run Number: 17203

Printed and bound in the United States of America.
BG 10 9 8 7 6 5 4 3 2 1

For Chase, who has the heart of a king.

Contents

Unless you already know how to save planet Earth from total destruction, read the next sentence of this book! Actually, this second sentence won't be all that helpful. Obviously not this third one either. Let's be honest, you'll probably need to read the entire book if you hope to learn anything useful.

In the first two books of Elliot's story, children were warned to stop reading as soon as possible. Recent scientific studies have shown that one in five readers obeyed the warning and put their books down right away. They have hidden in fear under their beds ever since, gratefully living off whatever crumbs were left behind by their kind mice friends.

Those readers who ignored the warning stepped into dangers they could not have foreseen. For example, at least twenty children read about Elliot while walking to school and accidentally stepped into potholes. This might not seem dangerous now, but if you continue reading this book, you will understand that holes of all sizes should be taken very seriously.

Even if you dared to read the other books about Elliot, this book's warning should not be ignored. In fact, if you care at all for planet Earth, you will pay very close attention to the lessons inside these pages. In past books, you were urged to close the book and run away. But now you are warned to turn the pages as fast as you can read them. You must know what happens inside this book to learn whether Earth gets destroyed. Because let's face it—that would be a bad thing.

If you cannot wait until the end of the book to find out if Earth has been destroyed, then here are a few tips to help you figure it out for yourself.

First, you should go to your kitchen cupboards and see if you have some peanut butter to make a sandwich. If you have no peanut butter, no cupboards, and for that matter, no kitchen, then it's possible that Earth was destroyed.

Second, you should ask your teacher when your homework is due. If she says it's not due until Friday because Earth was destroyed, then you will have your answer. Also, you won't have to worry about your grades anymore.

The final way to know if Earth has been destroyed is to look out your bedroom window. If you see planets and cosmos instead of plants and cars, then you are flying through space. This will mean that Elliot lost the war, and you will have to find a new planet to live on.

Hint: Choose a planet that has ice cream. You won't regret it.

Chapter 1

Where Mr. Beary-Boo Is Not Happy

It was a day Elliot Penster would remember for the rest of his life. Oddly, up until exactly 11:14 AM, it was a day Elliot would very much have liked to forget.

Because in all of his eleven years of life, Elliot had never had a day like this one. He had experienced some pretty unusual things, especially beginning last fall when he was made king of the Brownies. Since then, he'd been scared half to death by Goblins, had his house blown up, and had been kidnapped to the Underworld, where he ended up on an adventure that could change the course of world history. More about that later. Much, much more, in fact.

But as unusual as Elliot's recent life had been, somehow nothing was stranger than his being paired for a game of Capture the Flag with the scariest girl in the fifth grade,

Cambria Dawn Wortson, aka Cami with Warts On, aka Toadface.

For a long time, Elliot had felt that Cami must have inherited her looks from a toad somewhere in her family. But over the past winter she had gotten rid of her thick glasses that made her eyes look like melons with pupils, and she had stopped wearing clothes that made her look like a prison guard. Elliot's mother even commented that she thought Cami had become quite pretty over the winter. Elliot's sister, Wendy, said the only reason Elliot insisted he didn't like Cami was because he secretly *did* like her. That was ridiculous, of course. But at least he had stopped peeking at Cami's hands to see if the fingers were webbed like a toad's.

Over the past few months, Cami had decided that she and Elliot should do stuff together. Maybe even have fun at the same time. So apparently, they were friends now. Despite that, Elliot still considered Cami his number one arch nemesis.

Many readers of this book will be surprised to learn that Elliot's arch nemesis is Cami and not Kovol, the most evil Demon of all time.

Battling evil Demons wasn't Elliot's favorite thing about being king of the Brownies. He would have much preferred to drink Mushroom Surprise and sit on his royal toadstool in Burrowsville, where the Brownies lived. But nearly four months ago, he had awoken Kovol from his thousand-year nap. It was an accident, and the last thing Elliot had wanted to do, but he'd had no choice. Going to Kovol's cave in Demon Territory had been the only way to save his ex-bully, Tubs Lawless, from the Pixies, and his Brownie friend, Mr. Willimaker, from the Fairies. In revenge for what Elliot had done, Kovol had promised revenge on the entire human race. Good grief, Elliot thought. That had to be about the biggest overreaction of all time.

But one thing still kept Kovol from being Elliot's arch nemesis. For the past four months, Kovol had been stuck in a pit of gripping mud deep in the Underworld. He wouldn't be able to escape until there was a total eclipse of the sun. At that point, Kovol would probably move up to the number one position on Elliot's list of enemies.

Then Cami would have to slide down to number two, because, after all, she isn't trying to kill Elliot. She just really annoys him.

And she was especially annoying him today. Because when he showed up that morning to play a game of Capture the Flag in the woods behind his house, Cami had already picked him for her teammate. The other team wasn't much better. On that side was Tubs, who often got confused if he ever had to say more than two sentences in a row. Tubs was playing alone, because even he couldn't bully someone into being on his team.

"That's okay if I'm alone." Tubs pulled a stuffed teddy bear from his shirt. "Mr. Beary-Boo will guard our flag."

"Why do you have a teddy bear in your shirt?" Elliot asked.

"He's my best friend!" Tubs snarled. "Besides, there's two of you, so I need his help."

"We'll make you a deal," Cami said. "You let Mr. Beary-Boo guard your flag, and then we'll find something to guard ours. Then all of us will go out and try to steal the other team's flag."

And so the game began. Cami and Elliot found a small clearing surrounded by tall trees and thick bushes. They hid their flag in the dense branches of a maple tree while Tubs hid his flag somewhere farther away. "You start looking for the other flag," Cami told Elliot. "I'll get the guard for ours."

"Like what? Mr. Beary-Boo's long-lost teddy bear brother?" Elliot said. "You could have a dumb rock as guard for all it matters, because in case you didn't notice, Mr. Beary-Boo isn't real!"

Cami laughed. "You'd probably say Leprechauns aren't real either."

Elliot only shrugged. If Goblins and Elves and Pixies were real, then Leprechauns probably were too.

"Let's go!" Cami said. "Try to find his flag. I'll be back in a minute with our"—she stopped to giggle—"our guard!"

Elliot rolled his eyes and then began running. He used to

think these woods behind his house were sort of scary, so he'd always tried to avoid them. But then he had come face-to-face with Kovol, and nothing could ever be as scary as that.

He explored different areas where he was sure Tubs might have hidden the flag and listened carefully for any sounds that would tell him where Tubs was searching for his and Cami's flag. But all he heard was the wind brushing through the springtime leaves and the occasional chirp of a bird.

Then Elliot squinted in the distance. It was hard to know because of the shadows ahead, but he was pretty sure he saw Tubs's flag—an old green pillowcase—hanging from a tree.

Just hanging from a tree? Not hidden or disguised or anything?

Elliot smiled as he got closer. Tubs had put it near a clump of leaves. He probably hoped Elliot would think the pillowcase was just a really, really, really big leaf.

On the tree branch beside the pillowcase was Mr. Beary-Boo. Up close the teddy bear looked really old, and one of his button eyes was missing. No wonder he hadn't seen Elliot coming.

Laughing at his own joke, Elliot plucked the pillowcase off the tree. Now he had to get it back to his home base without being caught.

He turned to go and immediately ran right into Tubs's wide chest. Elliot bounced off it and landed on the ground.

"Mr. Beary-Boo thought you'd try something like this," Tubs said in a voice that reminded Elliot of the days when Tubs used to bully him. "Give me that pillowcase, or else."

Elliot swallowed hard. When Tubs talked like that, it always meant trouble. And trouble was the last thing Elliot wanted today.

Where the Sun Goes Dark

Tubs was the closest thing to a brick wall Elliot had ever run into (other than the brick wall he had run into a week ago when he forgot to watch where he was going). Now Elliot sat on the ground with the pillowcase flag in his hand.

"I said give me the flag, or else," Tubs snarled.

Elliot gripped the flag tighter. He wouldn't back down, no matter what Tubs threatened. "Or else what?" he asked.

Tubs frowned. "Or else I'll lose. Duh!"

Elliot rolled his eyes and got ready to run again. Tubs reached for the flag, but Elliot crawled between his widespread legs. Tubs kept bending lower to catch Elliot but ended up with his head behind his knees, then rolled into a somersault that left him flat on the ground.

Elliot leapt to his feet and ran toward his and Cami's base. "I've got it!" he yelled. "I've got it!"

Tubs crashed through the woods behind him, calling Elliot's name. At first he had laughed as he yelled for Elliot to slow down. Then his voice became angrier as he said, "Seriously. Give me the flag. I hate losing!"

"Me too!" Elliot answered. He wasn't far from their base now. He was easily going to win, and Cami hadn't done one thing to help. So he had beaten Tubs on his own!

Elliot ran into the clearing where their flag was still hidden. Then he stopped.

Cami had told him at least 120 million times over the winter that she had taken up paper-mache as a hobby. (Okay, maybe not quite that many times. But it was at least twice.) She had explained that this craft was as simple as dipping strips of paper in watered-down glue and putting them on a frame in whatever shapes she wanted. Then she had invited him over to her house to try it. "When it dries, you can paint it however you want!" she had said.

But Elliot had never wanted to try it. And he couldn't think of a single reason why he might ever want to in the future. Even if his life depended on it, he wouldn't have anything to do with Cami's paper-mache. So she told him that was fine, she would do her project without him.

And right now, beneath their hidden flag was their "guard." It was Cami's paper-mache project and was almost guaranteed to ruin his life once and for all.

It was a life-size version of him.

The worst part was that she had done a pretty good job. He had to get right up to its paper-mached face to know it wasn't really him.

"What do you think?" Cami bounced on her heels excitedly.

"Um." That was all he could think of to say. If he had ever known any other words, he couldn't think of even one.

"It's cool, right? I worked on it all winter and just finished it a week ago. I've been waiting for the perfect time to show it to you."

How could she possibly think *this* was the perfect time? And why did she have to carry that thing out in public? Everyone who saw it would know it was supposed to be him.

Behind Elliot, Tubs crashed into the clearing. He stopped right beside Elliot when he saw the paper-mache doll.

"You've got to be kidding," Tubs said.

Elliot closed his eyes. This was it. The beginning of the end (or the end of the beginning). The point when he wouldn't mind so much if the entire universe folded in half and squished him flat. Now Tubs would tease him and Cami about liking each other. Or sing rhymes using their names. Or make kissing noises when they walked by.

"I really don't believe it," Tubs added, walking closer.

"Do you like it?" Cami asked.

"It's so cool!" Tubs said. "I mean, whatever makes Elliot such a dork all the time, you really understood that when you made this. Great job!"

Elliot frowned. That might've been a compliment to Cami, but it wasn't to him.

Cami gestured at the doll. "What do you think?"

"It doesn't look anything like me," he said. "My hair is dark blond, not light brown, and my eyes aren't purple."

She giggled. "Yeah, but they're cooler that way."

"And I don't have a goofy, crooked smile," he continued.

"Sure you do," Cami said. "But this is my first try with life-size humans. Mostly I've been doing creature crafts."

Elliot's ears perked up. "What sort of creatures?" As king of the Brownies, he had to guard very carefully against anyone learning of the existence of mythological creatures. The Brownies were very sensitive about that.

"Oh, you'd love it! I just finished a model of a Goblin. He's tiny, and I painted him light pink. He's so cute!"

Elliot rolled his eyes. Goblins were not tiny or any shade of pink, and they definitely were not cute! If their leader,

Grissel, ever saw the model, he'd blow it up. And probably Cami's house along with it.

Seeing that Elliot was not impressed, Cami frowned and said, "I thought if you saw how cool this model was, you'd want to make some paper-mache creatures with me sometime."

"Um, no," Elliot said. Which was a very ordinary thing to say considering the very extraordinary thing that happened next.

Exactly when Elliot's watch turned to 11:14, the sunlight dimmed. It had been high in the sky when they started this game not too long ago.

Elliot forgot the flag in his hand and dropped it on the ground. It was as if night had suddenly decided to come all at once, even though it was still the middle of the day. "What's going on?" he asked.

"Oh, I forgot!" Cami rummaged through a bag slung over her shoulder. "There's a total eclipse of the sun today! I made a pinhole viewer so that we could watch it. Now, where— ah!" She pulled the pinhole viewer from her bag and showed it to Tubs and Elliot. "This is the only safe way to watch a solar eclipse."

As far as Elliot was concerned, there was nothing safe about a solar eclipse. Or at least, not *this* solar eclipse. Because as soon as the moon fully crossed in front of the sun, Kovol would be free.

Kovol had promised to destroy Earth once he escaped the gripping mud. Part of Elliot hoped that Kovol might have changed his mind while he was stuck in the mud. Maybe instead of getting revenge on Elliot, Kovol would celebrate his release by ordering some pizza. But the rest of Elliot understood that probably wouldn't happen. At least he couldn't think of any pizza places that delivered to the Underworld.

The eclipse created a strange light in the air. It wasn't true darkness, but more like everything had fallen into shadow. And with Elliot's mind on Kovol, the unusual light became even eerier.

A moment later the sun and moon had passed each other, and everything became normal again. It would've been an exciting moment if Elliot hadn't understood exactly what was now happening in the Underworld.

"Where are you going?" Cami asked him. "If you leave, we're gonna lose the game!"

"Mr. Beary-Boo will be so happy when I tell him we won!" Tubs said.

Elliot didn't care about the game or what Mr. Beary-Boo thought about anything. He was already sprinting home as fast as his long legs would carry him.

Kovol was free. And about to seek his revenge.

Chapter 3

Where the Earth Sinks

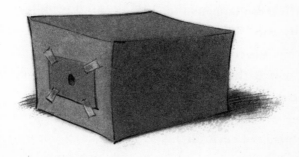

The door to Elliot's home banged open as he ran through
it. His sixteen-year-old brother, Reed, and fifteen-year-old
sister, Wendy, were sitting with their eyes glued to the television.
(They weren't actually *glued*, of course, because think of how
painful that would be! They were just watching it very carefully.)

"You were supposed to tell me if a solar eclipse was
coming," Elliot said to them. "You promised to warn me!"

Wendy turned to him. "Sorry, I forgot."

Sorry? Wendy would be plenty sorry when the entire world was destroyed.

Reed shrugged. "So you missed the eclipse. I missed free popcorn day at the zoo once. But you don't hear me complaining."

"That's not even close to the same thing!" Elliot said.

"You can see the next one," Wendy said. "It's no big deal."

"It is a big deal," Elliot insisted. "It happens to be about the biggest deal ever. Like the kind of big deal that means you won't cook dinner ever again!"

"It just so happens that I don't mind cooking anymore," Wendy said. "I haven't burned a single dinner in eight days."

"You burned the chicken nuggets last night," Reed said.

"I meant the eight days *before* last night," Wendy said. "My cooking is getting better lately."

This was mostly true. Her dinners still tasted like they were made of cornstarch and glue. But except for last night, at least it was unburned cornstarch and glue.

"Anyway, there's a much bigger deal than your missing the eclipse." Reed pointed to the television. "Look! About five minutes after the eclipse, this happened!"

Elliot walked closer to the TV screen. A reporter was standing in front of a road that had caved into the earth, as if it had been built on top of a giant sinkhole. It looked like Elliot's entire house could fit into that hole.

"Nobody knows what caused this unusual event," the reporter was saying. "And it's not the only one."

Other pictures of caved-in roads were shown on the screen. A few had cars at the bottom of them, and helicopters were being flown in to help pull the people out of the sinkholes.

The reporter continued, "Right now, every road into the town of Sprite's Hollow has caved in. Until they can be repaired, it will be very difficult for anyone to either come or go."

"What about Mom and Dad?" Wendy said. "They won't be able to get home from work!"

Reed shrugged. "They'll find a way home as soon as they can. But this is weird, right?"

It's not weird, Elliot wanted to shout. This was obviously Kovol's way of letting Elliot know he was free, and he was making sure Elliot had no way to leave Sprite's Hollow. But of course Wendy and Reed didn't know about Kovol or any part of the Underworld. So in a voice not too different from a shout, he asked, "Where are the twins? They shouldn't be outside right now."

Elliot's six-year-old twin brothers, Kyle and Cole, had a talent for getting themselves into trouble. Elliot figured that if sinkholes were appearing in Sprite's Hollow, his brothers were probably very near one. They'd love to fill a sinkhole with water to create a giant mud pit to play in.

"They're out gathering extra hoses," Wendy said. "They

want to make a super hose as long as Sprite's Hollow. But you're right. Come on, Reed. Help me find them."

As soon as they had left, another reporter came on the screen again. "More sinkholes have begun appearing outside of Sprite's Hollow," he said. "Dozens of new ones are being reported, some appearing as far away as China."

Dear Reader, if the reporter had said a sinkhole had appeared in Guatemala, this would not be much of a surprise, because they already have a giant sinkhole right in their capital city. It's over a hundred feet deep and big enough that it swallowed a three-story building. Nobody is sure exactly what caused that sinkhole, although scientists did eliminate the possibility of caved-in tunnels from freak-sized worms larger than rockets. Apparently, freak-sized worms don't exist. Besides, the reporter was very clear that this sinkhole was happening in China, not Guatemala. He pointed out that their fortune cookies would have to change to say, "Beware of walking into any holes larger than your house." Elliot thought most people would know that even without a fortune cookie's help. Except for maybe Tubs.

Once he made sure he was alone, Elliot ran up to his bedroom and closed the door. He put his hands around his mouth and shouted, "Mr. Willimaker!"

Mr. Willimaker was one of Elliot's closest Brownie friends and also his trusted advisor. Although it was true that most of

Mr. Willimaker's advice was not very helpful, Elliot also knew that nobody had tried harder to help him be a good king.

But after two long minutes of waiting, no one appeared. Elliot shook his head. Mr. Willimaker usually came very quickly. He called again, but before he finished calling, Mr. Willimaker's daughter, Patches, poofed in.

Despite being half Elliot's size, Patches's brown eyes were twice as big as human eyes. She had a small mouth and thick hair that went in all directions.

Patches had made it clear on every possible occasion that she thought Elliot was the greatest king the Brownies had ever had, and that he was about the greatest human in the history of the world. Elliot thought that last part was a bit of an exaggeration, but he was okay with letting her believe it.

As soon as she poofed in, Patches said, "I took a peek at your television news downstairs. Is that what it looks like on the surface?"

"I guess so. How does it look in the Underworld?"

"Worse. So far he's left Burrowsville alone, so the Brownies are fine. But it won't be long before he attacks us too." Patches widened her eyes. "Kovol's free now, Elliot."

"I know," he said. "But why is he making sinkholes?"

Patches bit her lip, and it looked as if she was trying hard not to cry. "He's collapsing the Underworld. He's going to destroy everything."

Chapter 4

Where Cami Walks In

Collapsing the Underworld," Elliot whispered. "Why would Kovol do that?"

"Because he's evil!" Patches replied, as if that was the only explanation needed.

Elliot shook his head. "I think that must be only part of the reason. With the Underworld in chaos, none of the good creatures will be able to help fight him. And those sinkholes will create a bunch of problems here on the surface. Because that's what Kovol really wants. To destroy the surface world."

Patches groaned and sat on Elliot's bed, her tiny legs dangling in midair. "This is bad. Worse than bad."

"Yeah." Elliot sat beside her and put his head in his hands. "Even though I knew he'd escape one day, I didn't think he'd act so fast."

He looked up at the sound of a poof, and Mr. Willimaker appeared, along with one of Elliot's other advisors, Fudd Fartwick. Never one to forget his manners, Mr. Willimaker bowed to Elliot. However, Fudd didn't bow. He'd been blinded when he helped to save Elliot from Kovol's army, the Shadow Men, four months ago. He didn't appear to have any clue where he was now.

"King Elliot," Mr. Willimaker said (and at that moment, Fudd did bow). "Sorry I'm late. There's a lot of trouble down below. You've heard the news, I assume."

"Do you mean the news that Kovol has escaped and is now collapsing the Underworld?" Elliot asked. "Or something else?"

Mr. Willimaker blinked. "Um, yes, that news."

"Just checking to be sure. Yeah, I heard. But I have another question first." Elliot turned to Fudd. "How are you doing?"

"Blindness is a bit of a challenge," Fudd said. "But at least I don't have to see my face in the mirror each morning!" He smiled as if he had tried to make a joke, but his voice still sounded sad.

"I'm sorry, Fudd," Elliot said. "It's my fault that happened."

Fudd looked directly at Elliot, or where he thought Elliot was, which meant he was actually looking at a bedpost. "King Elliot, sacrificing my eyesight was the least I could do in return for all you've done for me."

"Isn't there any way to fix your eyes?" Elliot asked. "I'd

think with all the magic in the Underworld, healing an injury like this would be easy."

"That's just it," Mr. Willimaker said. "Fudd's eyes weren't injured that day. They were cursed. The only way to undo a curse like that and heal Fudd is for a creature to give away all his magic."

"And I'd never let anyone to do that," Fudd said. "It's just too big a sacrifice."

They fell silent for only a moment before Wendy called from downstairs, "Elliot! Your friend Cami is here. She wants to apologize about some doll!"

"Tell her everything's fine and to go away!" Elliot yelled back.

"Can I send her up to see you?" Wendy asked.

It was hard to hear her because of the noise of the twins running around downstairs. Elliot was glad they had not fallen into some giant sinkhole, but now he had to yell back to his sister even louder.

"No way, no chance, never!" he answered.

"Okay!"

Elliot turned back to the Brownies. "All right, I need some ideas about how we can stop Kovol."

Suddenly, Patches and Mr. Willimaker disappeared. In the same instant, Elliot heard the creak of his door behind him.

Fudd must not have heard the door creak. Still looking at the bedpost, he said, "Your Highness, I think—"

He had spoken about four words too many and failed to disappear about four seconds too late.

"What is that?" someone asked.

Elliot turned and saw Cami in the doorway of his room. Her mouth hung open and her eyes were wide as she stared at Fudd. For a moment, Fudd looked as if he wanted to poof away, but then he must have decided there was really no point in that now.

Elliot groaned. What did Wendy think "no way, no chance, never" meant anyway: "Sure, send Cami right up"? With the noise the twins were making downstairs, she might not have heard him.

"Elliot, what is that?" Cami repeated, pointing at Fudd. "It's looking at me."

"*It* is a *he*, and he's my friend," Elliot said. "And he's blind, so he isn't actually looking at you, but he can hear you just fine and you're being rude."

"Oh. Sorry," Cami said. "But you still haven't told me what it—what...*he* is."

Elliot sighed. "Come back, Mr. Willimaker and Patches. I guess you can show yourselves now." Then he turned to Cami. "I've got a sort of big secret. Sit down and I'll tell you everything."

Chapter 5

Where Something Grabs Elliot's Gut

Cami's eyes got wider and wider while Elliot told her all about the existence of Pixies, Goblins, and other mythical creatures, and about how he had come to be the king of the Brownies.

"This explains a lot," Cami said. "Like why you've been such an odd kid for so many years."

Elliot arched his head. "I've only been the Brownie king since last fall."

"Oh," Cami said. "Well, this explains why you've been odder than usual since last fall."

She crouched down to Mr. Willimaker and shook his hand. "So Elliot's your king, huh?"

"He's been a great king," Mr. Willimaker said.

"The best," Fudd agreed.

Cami leaned over to get closer to Patches. "How old are you, little girl?"

Patches made a face. "Little? Are you saying I'm short?"

"Oh! Um, no! I'm sure you'll grow up to be a very big girl one day. Well…as big as Brownies ever get, which I guess is still little."

Elliot tried hard not to laugh. Cami probably didn't realize that Brownies live a lot longer than humans. Maybe Patches was the smallest in the room, but she wasn't the youngest—at least not in human years.

"So why are you here?" Elliot asked Cami.

"Well, you left the woods so fast that I was worried about you. And then my mom called, and she can't get home from work because of all the sinkholes." She shrugged. "I guess I was scared being there alone."

"Okay, but why would you come *here*?" Elliot repeated.

"Because we're friends. And friends help each other."

Oh, *that*. "My parents can't get home either, but I guess you can stay with us until your mom gets back," Elliot said. "In exchange, I need your help too."

"Sure."

He took a deep breath. "I'm going to the Underworld, at least to make sure the Brownies are okay, and then I'll decide what to do about Kovol."

"Thank you, King Elliot," Mr. Willimaker said softly.

Elliot continued, "I'm not sure how long I'll be gone, but until I get back you've got to cover for me with my family."

Cami clapped her hands together. "Oh, the Underworld? Fun! Can I come?"

And this was why Elliot didn't trust having girls for friends. First he had let her stay over because she was scared. Now she wanted to visit the Underworld with him. Next she'd decide they were best friends or something even worse. He wasn't falling into that trap! No way. He knew her tricks.

And besides, even if he wanted to bring her to the Underworld (which he definitely didn't), he needed her help up here.

"Who'll cover for me if you come with us?" he asked. "If my sister or brothers wonder where I am, I need you here to make an excuse for me so that they won't worry."

"Oh. Okay."

Cami looked so disappointed that he finally added, "You wouldn't want to come anyway. I might end up having to battle this evil Demon who wants to destroy Earth."

"Yeah, that old excuse," she said, waving her hand. "Fine, go battle your evil Demon. I'll just stay here and be bored."

"That's really why I'm going there," Elliot protested.

"Whatever. You didn't have time to make paper-mache animals, but you do have time to save the world."

Patches folded her arms and said, "He always has time for us."

Elliot looked at Mr. Willimaker as if to ask him why Patches was acting jealous. But Mr. Willimaker only shrugged and suggested they should leave. Quickly.

Looking at Elliot's bedpost again, Fudd said, "Your Highness, are you really coming to the Underworld with us?"

"It'll be dangerous," Mr. Willimaker warned.

"I know," Elliot said. "But I'm the one who woke Kovol up. If I can help anyone stop him, I will."

"Hold my hand," Fudd said to the bedpost. "That will be the safest way to poof."

Since the bedpost had no hands, and in fact had not answered Fudd even once, Elliot took Fudd's hand in his, then closed his eyes in dread of the next moment. He didn't like being poofed.

Then he cracked one eye open as Cami said, "Be safe, Elliot. If anyone can stop that Demon, you can."

Elliot started to thank her, but it was too late. The poofing magic grabbed on to his gut and yanked him away from his room. He was headed to the Underworld.

Chapter
6

Where It Begins

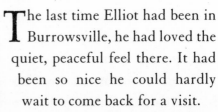

The last time Elliot had been in Burrowsville, he had loved the quiet, peaceful feel there. It had been so nice he could hardly wait to come back for a visit.

But things had changed. The small town was still quiet—too quiet, in fact. Not because it was peaceful, but because the fear was so thick in the air that nothing dared move. Even the usually gurgling stream through Burrowsville ran silently today.

Fudd, Patches, and Mr. Willimaker all stood beside Elliot at the top of a hill overlooking the town. In the distance of the Underworld, Elliot saw smoke and haze. The light down here was provided by the combined magic of all the Underworld creatures. But now it was dim and flickered on and off, as if the creatures were using their magic for hiding from Kovol rather than for lighting the Underworld.

"We're glad you came," Mr. Willimaker said as they began walking toward the center of Burrowsville.

"I wish I didn't have to come because of Kovol," Elliot said. "But I'm glad I'm here."

"You need to know about a power Kovol has," Fudd said. "A dangerous one. If he spreads his hands out wide"—Fudd demonstrated by holding his own hands apart—"like this, he's gathering his magic into that little space. It can hit you with the force of lightning."

"And that would be bad," Patches said.

"Don't get hit with a ball of lightning," Elliot said. "Good advice." He did a quick glance over the town. "It looks like Kovol's left Burrowsville alone."

"So far," Mr. Willimaker said.

The tiny mounds of homes with the paths between them were all in place, and their yards were as neat and orderly as always. But there were no Brownies working in their gardens or walking the winding paths of Burrowsville to visit with friends as they passed by. Now the town looked completely deserted.

Dear Reader, a deserted town is one where everyone has gone away and left it empty. Sometimes these are called ghost towns. A name like that can mean only one thing: ghosts must have chased everyone away.

If you have a ghost living in your town, there's no need for you to run away. There are ways for you and the ghost to become friends. You should start by doing things the ghost enjoys, such as floating around in attics. And moaning. Lots and lots of moaning.

Later you can invite the ghost to do fun things with you. Remember that some things will be tough for him, such as catching a baseball or swimming. And if you run a race, he'll probably win unless you can also fly to the finish line. But it'd be nice to let him win. After all, he's dead and you're not.

Finally, you should introduce the ghost to your friends. If you really want to have fun, suggest playing the game Ghosts in the Graveyard. When you bring the ghost out to play, everyone who doesn't faint with shock will enjoy a good laugh.

Elliot enjoyed playing games, but he definitely didn't feel like laughing right now. Besides, it didn't look like anyone was around to play with. He turned to Mr. Willimaker. "Where is everyone?"

"Hiding in their homes. We think it's only a matter of time before Kovol comes here to collapse Burrowsville."

"And if he does, then the Brownies will be trapped inside!" Elliot said. "Get them out to help me. We have to stop Kovol before he does anything to Burrowsville."

Mr. Willimaker and Patches bowed to Elliot and then poofed away to start gathering the other Brownies.

"He'll send the Shadow Men first," Fudd said. "Nobody knows how to fight them."

"I know how," Elliot said. "And you do too. We've already fought them once."

"I learned one thing," Fudd said. "Don't let a Shadow Man spit in your eyes and make you go blind."

"Definitely not," Elliot agreed. Actually, he didn't want anyone to spit in his eyes, no matter who they were.

Then Fudd snapped his fat fingers. "Light!"

"Exactly." Shadow Men couldn't touch direct light or they'd disappear in it. Elliot pressed his mouth tight and then opened it and said, "The Pixies promised to help us when Kovol escaped. It's time for their help. Fudd, I need you to bring the Pixie princess, Fidget Spitfly, here."

Fudd bowed to him and poofed away. At the same time, Elliot saw several Brownies already leaving their homes. They came out timidly at first, checking the sky to make sure it wasn't about to fall in on them (which is good advice for everyone, even if you're not being attacked by evil Demons, don't you think?). Then as more and more Brownies came out from their homes, they moved together in a big clump into the center of Burrowsville.

Elliot ran to the top of the hill near his toadstool throne. He could see hundreds of Brownies gathering, from tiny newborn Brownies all the way up to Brownies who were several hundred years old. All were dressed in simple, earth-colored clothes. Their wild gray hair was sticking up so much, it made them look even more frightened than they probably already were. Elliot still didn't know most of their names, but he thought of each one as his friend.

He waved his hands to get everyone's attention and said, "I know you're scared. You might be thinking that we have no chance. When I first became king, I wasn't sure we could stop the Goblins either. The Brownies had been losing that war for so long, we forgot that we are strong and clever and that we never give up! We won the Goblin war, and now we will fight Kovol and his Shadow Men. Whatever else happens, Kovol will *not* collapse Burrowsville while I'm king!"

Then he looked up as small bits of dirt landed on his head.

"What—" He jumped back as a large chunk of dirt fell on the ground, barely missing him.

"It's starting!" yelled a Brownie in front of the crowd.

"Burrowsville is collapsing!" another cried.

"Wait!" Elliot called. "I know about a kind of magic that all Brownies can do. You can make a cold fire in your hand. Get anything you have to hold that fire. Sticks or papers or anything made of wood! Surround Burrowsville with it, and then light the wood with the fire. The Shadow Men won't be able to cross it!"

"They can still collapse the town," a third Brownie cried.

"I'm taking care of that. Now move!" Elliot ordered.

Still in a panic, Brownies scurried in all directions. Elliot turned his back on them and called, "Fudd! What's taking so long?"

"Like, I had to do my hair!" a voice behind him said. "Totally chill out."

Elliot turned again. Fluttering in the air in front of him was the Pixie princess, Fidget Spitfly.

Where Elliot Steps into Shadow

Fidget was a foot high and looked about the same age as Elliot. Except she dressed like every flavor of fruit candy and had learned to speak Elliot's language by watching the totally awesomest television show ever, *Surfer Teen*. Her tiny wings were round, her ears were long and thin, and she had an explosion of curly yellow hair.

She and Elliot weren't exactly friends. But since it was Fidget's fault he had awoken Kovol, they had always known they'd have to work together one day to stop him.

Fidget held her hand out to examine her nails. "Oh, fruit

rot! I had to dodge a falling piece of the Underworld and broke a nail. Kovol's totally going to pay for this!"

"The Brownies need your help," Elliot said. "I need the Pixies to spread light all over Burrowsville so that we can keep the Shadow Men out. And if they try to collapse it, have the Pixies poof the chunks away before they fall."

"But what if the Shadow Men attack the Glimmering Forest while we're gone?" Fidget said. "My daddy wouldn't like that."

"We're testing this plan to see if it works," Elliot said. "Better to test it here than on your own home, right?"

Fidget tossed her hair back. "Totally!" She snapped her fingers and instantly hundreds of Pixies appeared. Then she announced, "We're going to make the awesomest ever dome of light to cover Burrowsville! For some strange reason, the Brownies actually like this place and want to keep it. Also, I'm making a scrapbook all about me. So if anyone takes my picture while I'm poofing away some collapsing pieces of the Underworld, that would be, like, totally and completely awesome!"

Together the Pixies flew up into the air. They separated until they were as wide apart as the distance they could spread their light. Once Fidget gave the order ("Okay, so like totally, y'know!"), within seconds a ceiling of light widened across all of Burrowsville.

Elliot kept an eye on the smoke as it continued moving

closer to Burrowsville. The Shadow Men were almost here. He hurried over to where the Brownies were building up kindling for their cold fires. They were working hard, but there was still too much to be done. Elliot joined the Brownies in piling up kindling, making sure there were no gaps.

"Hurry!" he said.

"Elliot!"

Surprised, Elliot jumped a little, then turned. When he saw who had come, he jumped again. He wasn't *surprised*, really. *Startled* might be a better word.

Dear Reader, even though the two words mean nearly the same thing, there is a very big difference between being surprised and being startled. Surprised is when it's your birthday and you get a large gift from your brother that you had not been expecting. Startled is when that gift turns out to be a giant python. It's a good thing that it's not necessary to explain what the word *horrified* means, because otherwise we would have to discuss that giant python swallowing your birthday party guests whole. The good news is there will be lots of birthday cake left for you. Surprise!

Unfortunately, it was not Elliot's birthday. And his brother probably wouldn't give him a giant python anyway, mostly because it wouldn't hold still long enough for Reed to wrap it. So when Elliot was startled, it was because Agatha the Hag had just appeared beside him.

Elliot had first met Agatha very soon after he became the Brownie king. In most ways she was the exact opposite of Fidget the Pixie. Fidget was young, fashionable, and beautiful. Agatha was older than dust and wore ragged clothes that were held together by little more than cobwebs. Her skin was dry and wrinkled, and she was dotted with warts. Worst of all, her left eye bulged out so far from her head, it seemed likely to fall out and land on him at any minute.

"I came to help," Agatha said. "It's about time the Underworld started fighting back."

"The Underworld has some powerful magical creatures," Elliot said. "Why aren't they fighting?"

"Nobody knows what to do. Kovol is stronger than any one of us. And we haven't had to work together for a thousand years."

"Not since the first Underworld war." Elliot remembered what the Brownies had taught him about the war that happened a thousand years ago when all the creatures of the Underworld had stood up to Kovol and the Shadow Men. "They worked together then, and now it's time we do that again."

As the last of the kindling was put into place, the Brownies used their magic to light cold fires on their hands and quickly set them on the kindling. Elliot had first seen Mr. Willimaker light a cold fire while they were on their way to Demon Territory one night. It was bright and gave off a little warmth, but it wouldn't burn on its own. As long as the Brownies used their magic to keep the fire alive and the Pixies kept the light above them, they could keep the Shadow Men out of Burrowsville.

Patches ran to Elliot. "We're ready. Are you sure this will work?"

"If everyone does their part, it'll work." Elliot started walking, keeping his eyes open for any dark holes in the dome. Agatha hobbled beside him on her cane.

"You don't have to be here," he said, thinking of how much older she looked and acted than when he'd last seen her. "You should rest somewhere."

"You forget that I'm really a beautiful young woman," Agatha said.

"Oh, right." Elliot hadn't really forgotten, but it was tough to look at her deep layers of wrinkles and remember that a woman even more beautiful than an angel was hiding inside.

"Besides, you might need me," Agatha added.

Before Elliot could answer, a Brownie far from them shouted, "They're here! The Shadow Men have come!"

Elliot ran toward the Brownie who had cried out. It was hard to see through the Pixies' light and the Brownies' fire, but sure enough, an entire army of Shadow Men was on the other side, ready to attack.

Elliot's gut did a belly flop as he stood frozen for a moment. He'd faced Grissel the Goblin and a Shapeshifter posing as a werewolf, and even Cami Wortson when she was mad at him. But he feared the Shadow Men most of all.

Shadow Men were made of smoke and a black fire that burned but gave off no light. They wore long black cloaks that held the fire in, but thick smoke poured out from beneath the cloak in every direction and could choke a person who got too close. They smelled of charcoal and cinders and spoke with a hissing sound that made Elliot's skin crawl.

A Shadow Man in front tried to push through the dome of light but screeched as it stung his hand, and he pulled back. Another two or three tried to get past the Brownies' fire, but they failed too.

"It's working!" one of the Brownies said.

"Keep your guard up," Elliot said as the Shadow Men grouped together and flew to another area of the dome. "They'll keep testing us and trying to find a way in."

"They're over here," several Brownies a long way from Elliot called. "King Elliot, please come!"

Elliot took a breath, then began running. It would be a very long, very tiring war if he had to run everywhere all the time.

He turned to tell Agatha that, but she had already poofed herself there. By the time Elliot came, the Shadow Men were trying to break through the light dome again. Luckily, the Pixies held their magic strong, and no Shadow Man could push through it.

Elliot bent over to catch his breath, but other Brownies from even farther away cried, "Now they're over here!"

Between breaths, Elliot wondered why the Shadow Men had to fly so far away each time. Couldn't they just test the light dome all in one place so that it wasn't so tiring? It was like they wanted to make this war tough on him or something.

"I'll be right there," Elliot panted. He started to run, then leaned over with his hands on his knees and said to Agatha, "Will you go tell them to stay strong?"

Agatha nodded and poofed away. When his breath slowed, Elliot hurried toward the latest cry for help.

Then he stopped as his foot stepped into a shadow.

Shadow? There couldn't be shadows in here. The entire town was bathed in light from all directions. A shadow was bad.

High above him he saw a small gap of darkness. A Pixie fluttered in the center of it. He wasn't sure what she was doing, but her hands were moving behind her head.

"Get your light back," he called up to her.

"In a minute. But I have to tie my hair back first," she said. "You won't believe how much wind the Shadow Men are making out here."

"Light!" Elliot cried.

"Fine!" She lowered her hands and shook her hair out. "But if I get a tangle in my beautiful hair, it's all your fault."

"Light!" Elliot repeated. She huffed and spread her light again, but it was too late. Five cloaked shadows made it through the gap just in time. A sixth one made it halfway through, but the light cut him off and he disappeared.

The five Shadow Men swept down through the air in a flight that reminded Elliot of a hawk diving for its prey. Smoke trailed from their cloaks like a damaged airplane about to crash land. But these creatures weren't damaged and weren't going to crash. In fact, the closer they flew to Elliot, the darker the fire inside their cloaks burned. Then at once, all five of them looked at Elliot and flew even faster. They were arrows, and he was their target. All he could see was the smoke of their bodies and the raging black fire inside their cloaks.

They were coming straight for Elliot.

Chapter 8

Where Fire Burns

Elliot stumbled back a step and looked around for anything he might use to defend himself from the approaching Shadow Men. But there was nothing. Everything that could hold light had been carried to the borders.

The Shadow Men stopped directly in front of him and spoke: "King Elliot of the Brownies." He couldn't see their faces, so it wasn't clear exactly which of them was talking. It sounded like they were all speaking at the same time. If they weren't his enemies who were about to attack him, he'd have asked how they all knew what the others wanted to say. Because the answer was probably pretty cool.

"Get out of here while you still can," Elliot warned. He had tried to sound brave, but it felt like something inside his belly was doing somersaults.

They took a step forward and all said, "You will serve Kovol forever or else pay the price of doom."

Elliot snorted, not sure exactly what the going price for doom was these days. "No way! I'll already be in trouble if my mom finds out I'm down here fighting an Underworld war without permission. Can you imagine if she found out I promised to serve some ugly super villain?"

They laughed, all of them with the exact same laugh. Which would have been fine if Elliot had told a joke. But he hadn't. So it was actually sort of creepy.

"Then you will be the first human Kovol destroys," they said. "Leave with us now, and save this place from doom."

Sheesh, Elliot thought. The Shadow Men really had a thing for doom. Although he very much liked the idea of their leaving, no way was he going with them. His family had a very strict rule about never going anywhere with strangers. And even if they didn't have the rule, Elliot knew that leaving with the Shadow Men was a terrible idea.

Elliot's hands folded into fists. "I said to leave while you still can."

"We'll only leave with you as our prisoner."

Elliot shook his head. "You're trapped inside this dome of light. I think that *you* are *my* prisoners."

Another laugh, even creepier this time. Then the Shadow Men spread out, surrounding him. They flew to their left, faster and faster, swirling around Elliot. He sank to the ground as they pulled air away from him, sucking it from his lungs. He was really scared but also sort of annoyed. They were supposed to be his prisoners, yet he was the one who was trapped. This wasn't fair!

Elliot should have been used to things in his life not being fair. It wasn't fair that when he was five, Tubs stole his sandwich every day for a whole month and he had to eat napkins for lunch. It wasn't fair that his house had been blown up by the Goblins, or that day when Wendy had accidentally shaved the middle of his head and given him a backward Mohawk. But somehow this not-fair moment seemed worse than all the others combined.

Just as Elliot felt the last of his air being sucked away from him, the Shadow Men let out a pained screech as in their swirling three of them crashed into a wall of light. Air filled Elliot's lungs again and he looked up. Agatha had transformed into her angel self and, with her hands held high, created a light so white it hurt his eyes.

Her wobbly cane was still in her hands, but now it was as bright as the sun. It created a line above her head that seemed to give the Shadow Men pain if they came anywhere close to it.

Elliot stood and ran to where the Shadow Men could hear him. "Tell Kovol to go back to Demon Territory and stop this war," he warned. "If he doesn't, we will defeat him."

"You're only a human," the last two Shadow Men said. "We'll tell Kovol nothing for you."

"Fine! Then he'll find out on his own!" Elliot threw up his hands and began walking away. Add stubbornness to the list of things he didn't like about Shadow Men.

"Elliot, look out!" Agatha cried.

Before Elliot turned, he felt the hot claw of a Shadow Man grab his shoulder. Even through his shirt he felt its burn.

"Catch this!" Agatha tossed her cane at him, and Elliot ripped free and dove for it. As soon as it was in his hands, he swerved around and struck the Shadow Man in the chest. It screeched for only an instant before its cloak dissolved and fell like ashes at his feet.

"This is over for now, but we'll be back," the remaining Shadow Man said. "And next time it won't be so easy for you."

He fled up in the air toward the light dome. He tried to push through it but disappeared, as shadows will. Nothing came through on the other side. Seeing what had happened inside the dome, the Shadow Men on the outside quickly flew away.

Suddenly tired, Elliot fell to his knees. Agatha crouched beside him. "Are you okay?"

"Sure," he mumbled. The shoulder of his shirt was burned off, and the skin below it was hot and red, but he couldn't worry about that right now. "What happened to that Shadow Man I hit?"

"Kovol cursed the fire to create an army from the flames," Agatha said. "That Shadow Man was nothing but smoke and ash."

"They said it won't be as easy next time," Elliot said. "Did they think this was easy?"

"There will be more battles," Agatha said. "And the next one will get much worse."

Chapter 9

Where Everyone Arrives

When the last of the Shadow Men had flown away, a cheer rose up from the Brownies. Mr. Willimaker ran toward Elliot, then stopped and bowed before he said, "You did it, Your Highness! You saved us!"

"Only for now," Elliot said. Fidget fluttered down from above them. Her thick mass of hair looked wind-tossed and wasn't nearly as bouncy as usual.

"I hope you know that was a lot harder than it looked," Fidget said. "They were, like, so totally mean!"

"But you were...um...awesome," Elliot said. "We couldn't have done this without the Pixies."

Fidget arched her head in pride. "Totally. But now we're even, right? We don't owe each other anything more."

"It's not about being even," Elliot said. "It's about stopping Kovol."

Fidget frowned. "Oh, fruit rot! If I have to fight in a war to save the world, then I'm totally going to miss *Surfer Teen* on TV tonight." She punched a fist into her palm. "If Kovol wants to destroy the Underworld, then that's totally rude. But now he's ruining the awesomest TV show ever, and the Pixies will not allow that!"

Elliot stood and said to Fidget, "I'll help whoever wants to lead this war. But I need some time to think of ideas about how to fight it. Meet me back here later and we'll talk about it."

"What if anyone else wants to come?" she asked.

"If they're willing to fight against Kovol and save the Underworld, then I want them to come!"

After Fidget left, Elliot asked for a place where he could think in private. Mr. Willimaker suggested Burrow Cave, and then Patches offered to walk Elliot there.

"I think I can find it," Elliot said. Burrowsville wasn't

that big, and they only had one cave large enough for all the Brownies.

"I know," Patches said. "But I thought you'd want some company."

She was right. He did.

"How's your shoulder?" Patches asked.

"It hurts a little." Actually it hurt a lot. The Shadow Man had been so angry when he grabbed Elliot that his fire had been very hot.

"Kneel down," Patches said.

As he did, Patches walked behind him and rubbed her hands together. "Are you going to heal it with magic?" Elliot asked.

"Not everything is magic," Patches said with a giggle. Then she peeked over his shoulder and began pasting it with something bright green and sticky that smelled like the inside of Reed's old shoes.

"What's that?" Elliot turned his head and quickly faced forward again. Coming too close to that stuff made his nose hurt.

"Pumpkin guts and tree moss and that stuff that sometimes collects on the edges of ponds. It makes a great burn paste." Patches shrugged. "I figured we'd need it, seeing as we were fighting fire and all."

"Thanks, Patches." Elliot gently touched the burn. The pain was already going away. "You really are smart."

"Not just ordinary smart," she said. "I'm super smart!"

Elliot chuckled. "Maybe you're smart enough to figure out how to beat Kovol."

She shook her head. "Nobody's *that* smart." Then she stopped, realizing what she had said. "Oh! I mean except you, right?" She pointed ahead to Burrow Cave. "Here we are! Go in and be super smart too."

"Thanks." The cave wasn't quite big enough for him, but it was the biggest private place the Brownies had. Being the super-smart king of the Brownies that he was, he tripped over a root at the entrance. Then he picked himself up and, without looking back to see if anyone was laughing, walked the rest of the way into the cave.

By the time Fudd called for him a while later, Elliot had decided for sure that Kovol needed to be defeated, and he was double sure he didn't want Earth destroyed. But the details of how someone might stop Kovol were still a little fuzzy. All in all, he hadn't gotten nearly as much thinking done as he had hoped for, and he certainly didn't feel super smart.

"Everyone's waiting for you," Fudd said, walking beside Elliot.

"Everyone?" That sounded like a lot.

It *was* a lot. Maybe five times what he had expected. Crowded into the small open space of Burrowsville were hundreds of creatures of every kind. He thought Fidget was inviting only *some* of her friends.

Near the front were the Dwarves, the full-grown ones about Elliot's own height. They had long, thick beards and strong bodies. Most of them had picks or axes or other mining tools slung across their backs. Behind them stood a herd of half-human, half-horse Centaurs. They were large and muscular with bare chests and hair hanging past their shoulders. Their ears were slightly pointed and high on their head, as if unable to decide whether to be human or horselike, so they settled on something in between. Behind the Centaurs were several Trolls, including one who had half of his fist shoved up his nose in search of something there. Elliot recognized the Fairies up in the air, along with a couple of other flying creatures he didn't know. There were also Elves and a few Yetis, and Satyrs, and even some Mermaids near the banks of the river running through Burrowsville. All waiting for him.

"There are so many," Elliot whispered.

"They came to hear your plan," Fudd replied. "They came to fight Kovol."

The crowd quieted when they saw Elliot. He sat on his toadstool throne and looked them over. These were magical creatures who were smarter than him—and mostly bigger than him.

"Why me?" Elliot asked no one in particular. "I said I would help. But am I supposed to lead this battle?"

"You are our king, and they've chosen you as their leader," Fudd said. "You've defeated the Goblins and gotten past Kovol and his army once before. You're the only one who can help us win this."

Elliot took a deep breath. As he looked around the crowd, he wondered how that could be true. Maybe it wasn't about who was most capable of winning but who was most willing to try. He stood again and shoved his hands into his pockets. He knew that didn't look very kinglike, but he didn't care about looking like a king right then.

"Um, I don't know what to say," Elliot began. "I guess I'm open to any ideas."

A murmur spread through the crowd. Several creatures turned their backs on him, ready to leave.

"Your Highness, they need more than that," Fudd said. "They're here to follow you, but you must show them that you can lead this."

"But I'm not sure that I *can* lead this," Elliot said. "I'm just a kid."

"I know you can, because you're our king," Fudd said. "It's okay if you don't believe that yet. But make *them* believe it."

"I'll try." Elliot raised his hands and started over. "A thousand years ago, Kovol was defeated the first time. It was your parents and grandparents and great-grandparents who fought him before, who made the Underworld safe for us. Now it's our turn. We will beat him again, *if* we are willing to fight him together."

This time the crowd cheered, but Elliot didn't feel much better. That speech had been the easy part. Now he was supposed to tell them how it would happen.

"What are you really good at?" Elliot continued. "Look at your strengths. Figure out how you can use them against Kovol."

"We're good at light," Fidget said, fluttering to the front of the crowd. "But nobody knows where Kovol will go next. We can't build a light dome over the whole Underworld."

A Dwarf stepped forward. "The Shadow Men could grab us before our short arms will ever reach them. But we can build defenses for others to use in their fights."

The Troll with the finger up his nose ambled forward as if he wanted to say something. But then he blinked as if his finger had pushed into his brain, and he stepped back into place.

Don't worry about his brain, Dear Reader. He'll barely notice a difference.

"Anyone else?" Elliot asked.

A large bird that had been in the air landed on the ground, spun around, and turned into a human boy Elliot recognized. This was his friend Harold, a Shapeshifter who had helped save Elliot on the night he woke up Kovol.

"You know my strengths," Harold said. "Just tell me what you want, and I'll do it."

"And me," said a Centaur in the back of the crowd.

"And me," added a Mermaid from the river.

"Okay." Elliot looked around. His mind raced as he looked the crowd over. He started with the Fairies. "We need everyone we can get on our side. Will you gather as many creatures as you can? Tell them we must fight together, or we'll each face the collapse of the Underworld alone."

The Fairies nodded, then vanished. Elliot next turned to Fudd. "You've worked with the Goblins once before. If anyone can convince them to help us, it's you."

"The Goblins only promised not to hurt us," Fudd said. "But they won't help us unless their leader, Grissel, agrees. And he's still in our Brownie prison, having to eat that horrible chocolate cake." He shivered just thinking of it.

"No more chocolate cake," Elliot said. "Bring him the biggest jar of pickles you can find, and tell him I want his help. He still has to promise not to hurt the Brownies, but there's nobody as good at blowing things up as Grissel."

Fudd dipped his head at his king. "Yes, Your Highness." Then he poofed away.

Harold stepped forward. "And what about me? Can I help?"

Elliot took a deep breath, then nodded at the Shapeshifter. "I need you for one of the biggest jobs of all. I need you to turn into me again and let Kovol see you down here. When he does, he'll chase you. If he gets too close, change into a butterfly, or a bumblebee, or something he won't suspect and can't catch. Keep him confused but busy and distracted. And whatever you do, keep him far, far away from Demon Territory. Can you do that?"

Harold paled a little, as if he were already shapeshifting into a white snowman. Then slowly he returned to his normal color. He swallowed hard, then nodded. With a squeak, he said, "I thought you'd ask me to bring chips and dip for the battle, or do something simple. But I said I would help, and I will."

He closed his eyes and shapeshifted into a bird again. Before he flew off, he tweeted back to Elliot, "If I don't come back, make sure to tell the love of my life, the beautiful Cami Wortson, that I was a hero."

"Of course you'll come back," Elliot said. "And for the last time, she's not the love of your life!"

When Harold had flown away, Mr. Willimaker stepped forward from the crowd and asked, "What good will it do to send Kovol away from Demon Territory? None of us are there, so neither is he. We have to defend our homes out here instead."

Elliot smiled. "We're not going to defend ourselves from Kovol. We're going to attack."

Chapter 10

Where Elliot Meets Slimy Toe Jam

Dear Reader, at one time or another, you have probably played a sport such as tennis or basketball, or Limburger soccer. (It's pretty much the same as regular soccer, except that you kick around a chunk of stinky Limburger cheese instead of a ball. The only downside is that it smells so bad, nobody really wants to get anywhere near it.) If you have, then you know it's very important to have a strong defense, or the other team will score points and win the game. But it's even more important to have a good offense, or plan of attack. Because if you don't, you'll never earn any points for your team. A defense only stops you from losing. To win, you have to attack.

And Elliot understood this. His family had played an exciting game of Limburger soccer only one week before. His twin brothers had won the game, in part because they didn't mind bad smells. And also because they cheated.

The rest of the mythical creatures didn't understand the reasons for attacking Kovol quite as well as Elliot did. (Limburger cheese is very hard to find in the Underworld—and that's a good thing.)

When Elliot announced his plan to the group, everyone got very quiet. The Troll in the back did jump up and say "Yay!" but Elliot soon realized it was because he had finally found what he'd been reaching for in his nose, not because he liked the idea of attacking Kovol.

"Why would we go to Demon Territory?" a Fairy asked. "That's Kovol's land."

"Exactly," Elliot said. "If we fight him in our own lands, then he will destroy them. But if we can beat him in Demon Territory, then we'll win this war."

"If Kovol catches us in his territory, he can make us his prisoner," an Elf said.

"I doubt that, because he's not a king," Elliot said. "And besides, he won't know we're there until we're already winning."

The moans continued, but Elliot said, "Everyone go home and gather the rest of your kind. Come as soon as you can to Demon Territory."

There were a handful of grumbles, at least twenty-two growls, and one rather high-pitched whine. But they had chosen Elliot to lead this war and intended to obey him. One by one the various groups poofed themselves away.

Except for the Elves. They waited until everyone had left before one came forward. He was a tall and handsome Elf with long white hair that fell like silk down his back.

"I am Slimmy Tojam," he said.

Elliot blinked. Had that elf just said he had slimy toe jam? If a Dwarf or a Troll or a Goblin had said that, then he could understand. But he wouldn't have thought any type of slime would be a problem for an Elf.

"You're slimy?" Elliot asked.

"It's Slimmy. Like Timmy or Jimmy. And it's my name, not a description of my feet."

"Toe Jam?"

The elf looked annoyed. "Tojam. Not 'jam,' like one spreads on toast, but 'jum,' that rhymes with 'come.'"

The fact that his name sounded like foot fungus made Elliot giggle. However, Mr. Tojam was a very serious-looking Elf and didn't seem to think his name was nearly as funny as Elliot did. So Elliot apologized. He hadn't meant to be rude. It's what he really thought the Elf had said.

"I am a teacher among the Elves," Mr. Tojam said.

Elliot wondered what the kids at his school would say if someone named Slimy Toe Jam started teaching there. They once had a teacher whose name was Mrs. Popzitt. She left after only three weeks to teach on an island where the natives all spoke in sign language, and she hadn't been seen since. Nobody blamed her for leaving.

"You've been thinking about my name for a long time," Mr. Tojam said. "Can we move on?"

"Oh, yeah, sure."

Mr. Tojam held up a book for Elliot to see. It looked very old and dusty, and the pages were wrinkled. "Now, what do you know about Kovol?"

Elliot shrugged. "I know he's the most evil Demon of all time. I know that a thousand years ago, in the first Underworld War, a wizard named Minthred cast a spell that put Kovol to sleep." Elliot also knew from having once been very close to Kovol's wide-open mouth that he had really bad breath. Or maybe that was only Kovol's morning breath. Probably not worth mentioning.

"The Elves believe the only way to defeat Kovol now is to

understand how he was defeated the first time." Mr. Tojam held out his arm, inviting Elliot to walk with him. "Is there a private place we can talk?"

Elliot glanced over at Mr. Willimaker, who suggested they return to Burrow Cave. Then Patches reminded her father that Elliot could only barely sit up in the cave, and Mr. Tojam was even taller than him.

"Allow me." Mr. Tojam touched Elliot on his shoulder and then closed his eyes. Elliot felt the tug on his gut poofing him away, but the Elf was a much better poofer than either the Brownies or the Pixies, and Elliot barely felt a thing. They arrived on a thick tree branch very high above the ground, but Elliot was so comfortable in that spot that he didn't worry a bit about falling. Besides, he had much bigger worries on his mind. Such as accidentally calling Mr. Tojam by the wrong name again. Or the end of the world, for example.

Mr. Tojam handed Elliot the book and opened it to the first page. It was an old and faded drawing of Kovol as he would have looked a thousand years ago. Sure enough, he had a full head of Demon hair. No wonder he had been upset when Elliot pulled out the last hair, making him bald. But as everyone knows, baldness is just one of the risks when taking thousand-year naps. Also, your favorite show might not be on television anymore (if television even exists still!).

In the picture, Kovol was facing an army of mythical

creatures that were not too different from those Elliot had just spoken to. In fact, right at the front was a Brownie who looked a lot like Mr. Willimaker. Elliot knew Mr. Willimaker's great-grandfather had fought Kovol before. He wondered if the Brownie in the picture was him.

"It was a terrible war," Mr. Tojam said. "Nobody had ever faced a creature such as this, and nobody had any idea of what to do."

"What made Kovol so much worse than any other Demon?" Elliot asked. "And why is he the last of them?"

"That was Kovol's plan," Mr. Tojam said. "All Demons have a certain amount of bad inside, but it had never been difficult for any of the good creatures to keep control of them. One day Kovol got into a fight with another Demon about who would get the last slice of dessert."

"Seems harmless enough." Elliot and his brothers often fought for that same reason. Unless Wendy had cooked it. Then they fought over who would have to choke it down and not hurt her feelings.

Mr. Tojam shook his head. "It should have been harmless, except that the other Demon ate the dessert first. In a rage, Kovol then picked up the Demon and ate him."

"Eww." There had not been a single fight in Elliot's home in which he had ever considered eating his brothers. Seriously. Not even once.

"As soon as Kovol ate him, he realized that he had taken the Demon's powers into his own body. In that moment, Kovol became stronger. And far more greedy. He wanted more and more power, and so he continued eating others of his own kind. With each meal, he grew stronger and more wicked. One by one, he destroyed every other Demon of the Underworld. Until he was the last."

As he spoke, Mr. Tojam turned the pages of the book, each picture showing Kovol becoming larger and stronger. Then he turned the page again, which showed Kovol in front of a wall of black fire.

"Kovol then turned his eyes upon the rest of the Underworld," Mr. Tojam continued. "For although he had the strength of all the Demons, he did not have the power of other magical creatures. Not the wisdom of the Fairies, or the grit of the Dwarves, or any of the special gifts the rest of the Underworld creatures have. So began the first war of the Underworld."

"You had to fight it," Elliot whispered. "Because he wouldn't stop until everyone was destroyed."

"But Kovol needed an army." Mr. Tojam tapped the picture again. "He couldn't have an army of living creatures, because he knew he'd end up eating them too, to take their power. So he cursed the fire, and from it came the Shadow Men. They are nothing but smoke and flame, and they have no thought other than to obey Kovol's will."

Elliot went to turn the next page and learn more, but Mr. Tojam stopped him. "The last page of this book is for your eyes only," the Elf said. "This is the wizard Minthred's own journal. He knew that one day Kovol would awake, and when he did, someone would have to lead the fight against him. He asked that the last page be read only by that person—by you. The Elves believe that everything you must know to defeat Kovol will be on that page. Call to me when you're finished, and I'll return you to the Brownies."

Mr. Tojam closed his eyes and poofed away, leaving Elliot alone at the top of the tree. This was great news. If the secret to winning the war was in this book, he could have it ended by dinner. Feeling very happy, Elliot blew out a puff of air and then turned the page.

The very first words he read were, "My name is Minthred, but I'm no wizard. And I don't know how I defeated Kovol."

Where Minthred Likes Goats

If Elliot had not been delicately balanced at the top of a very tall tree, he might have stood up and banged Minthred's journal as hard as he could against the branches. What did Minthred mean by saying he wasn't a wizard? From the very first moment Elliot had heard about Kovol, it was that the *wizard* Minthred had defeated him. And how could Minthred not know how he had done it?

However, since Elliot didn't want to lose his balance by beating up the journal, he only took another deep breath and then read further.

"I'm a poor goat herder," Minthred wrote.

"Oh, good grief," Elliot mumbled. Of course he was.

"Goat herding is a simple life and sometimes a very lonely life. (Which you can probably understand, Dear Reader. Goats rarely have anything interesting to say.) One day, large craters appeared in my field, as if the earth had sunk. In some places they were as large as an entire row of homes. While I was out studying them, thousands of creatures suddenly appeared, most of which I had thought were nothing but the inventions of storytellers. Yet here they were, standing in my field, and not only standing, but fighting an army of smoke and fire. At the center of it all was the terrible beast I now know is named Kovol."

Elliot closed his eyes and tried to picture what that must have looked like to Minthred. He remembered how surprised he had been when he first saw the Brownies standing in his bedroom, and there were only three of them. Minthred's surprise must have been a lot bigger. And a lot worse.

"I hid in my bed for a while," Minthred wrote. "But one

cannot hide from anything so awful for long. Besides, my goats were afraid too, and we couldn't all fit under the blanket."

Elliot scrunched up his face. He wouldn't invite a whole herd of goats to share his bed, whether they'd fit in there or not. No matter how scared they were.

Minthred continued, "I was finally forced to leave the safety of my bed, mostly because my goats ate the blanket. I knew that to face the war I needed the courage that would only come from a tall cup of turnip juice with just a bit of goat spit in it."

Elliot smiled. The Brownies also loved turnip juice, although he didn't think they added any goat spit to theirs. At least, he *hoped* not. Ick! Then he kept reading.

"But when I came to the battle, the Demon Kovol saw my drink. He smelled the turnip juice and roared that he was thirsty. His roar was so loud that all the earwax popped from my ears and fell into the cup. I dropped it and ran for my life. Kovol picked up the cup and drank it. All I know is that after drinking, he fell to the ground, fast asleep. The creatures cheered for me and said that I must be the finest of all wizards. They were so happy, I couldn't tell them I was only a simple goat herder, and that I had no idea why Kovol fell asleep."

And that was it. The last of the entry. The secret page that the Elves believed contained some all-powerful plan to defeat Kovol. What would they think if they knew that page had been written by some goat herder whose only magical power seemed to be the gift of producing an extreme amount of earwax?

Elliot slammed the book shut and then called for—how did he pronounce that again? Not Toe Jam. Maybe he could just call the Elf by his first name. Was it Slimy? Elliot groaned. If he couldn't remember the Elf's name, how could he possibly call him to come back and return Elliot to Burrowsville?

Chapter 12

Where Elliot Stops

Elliot waited in the tree for a moment before someone finally poofed up to see him. Only it wasn't the Elf.

It was Fidget, carrying a mirror in one hand and her wand in the other. She briefly glanced at him before returning to study herself in the mirror. "We're about to fight a war, and you're up here reading?" she asked.

He looked at the book. "The Elves gave it to me. But it wasn't very helpful."

"I could've told you that!" Fidget said.

"Why? Have you read it?"

Fidget scrunched up her nose. "Hello? Does it look like I read totally boring, thousand-year-old books?"

"I didn't think you read any books at all," Elliot said.

Fidget rapped him on the head with her wand for that,

then said, "I happen to read the awesome magazine *Totally Awesome Teen*, and it is totally awesome. Your book is obviously a waste of time, because if it had anything important to say, Minthred would have covered it in pink glitter!"

She touched her wand to the book, which disappeared from his hands. "Hey!" he said.

"I sent it safely under your pillow at home. If you want to be bored, then read it there." Her eyes flicked up and down Elliot's body in disapproval. "You totally don't look like someone ready to lead an Underworld war," she said. "I mean, half your shirt is burned. And there's stuff on your shoulder that turned your skin green."

It was the paste that Patches had put on his burn from the Shadow Man. But Elliot wasn't in the mood to explain that to a Pixie princess. Actually, he didn't want to explain to anyone why his skin was green.

"Go away," he said. "I'm waiting for that Elf who brought me here. Do...do you remember his name?"

"It's Slimmy Tojam." Fidget closed one eye to magically dab a little color on the lid with her wand. Then a draft of wind tossed her up in the air, and she poked herself in the eye. Her eye turned pink, the color she had planned to put on her lid. "Ow!" she said. Then she did a quick check in the mirror. "Oh, groovy! I look so awesome."

"What about Mr. Tojam?" Elliot said.

"Oh. He's not coming back."

"Why not?"

She sighed. "Obviously, I sent him away. You'll have to get back to Burrowsville on your own."

"I can't—"

"Sure you can." Fidget lowered her mirror. "Do I have to explain everything to you, human?"

Elliot rolled his eyes. "You haven't explained *anything* to me."

"Oh, that's right." Fidget giggled and turned almost as pink as her eye. "How totally embarrassing! Well, here's the TBNN—totally brand-new news. It's the awesomest news you've probably ever had." Her tiny nose wrinkled. "Well, let's be honest. You probably don't get a lot of awesome news. I mean, your family doesn't even have enough money to give you a shirt without a hole in the armpit. And you've had a bully for almost as long as you've been alive. And you're king of the Brownies, who are, like, the lamest creatures ever when it comes to styling their hair. So I could probably tell you anything, and it would still be better than your usual news."

Elliot was tired of this. "What's the news, Fidget?"

She huffed. "Well, if you *are* going to lead us through this Underworld war, then the Pixies will help. And we thought, what is the awesomest thing we could do for you?" Her face brightened. "I'm the one who thought of this idea!

I'm so proud of me." Then for no clear reason, she playfully punched Elliot in the arm, which hurt a lot, considering that her whole body was only the size of his arm. "How lucky are you that we're friends?"

"Obviously, the luckiest kid in the universe," Elliot muttered. "Now, what's the news?"

Fidget waved her wand and glitter poured all over him. It tingled and even tickled wherever it landed. He tried to brush it off, but that only rubbed it into his skin.

"Yay!" Fidget exclaimed.

"That's your big surprise?" Elliot asked. Whatever the glitter was for, it had come from the Pixies. Which meant he didn't like it, or trust it, even one bit.

Fidget frowned, clearly disappointed that he was not impressed. "Fine. If you don't care about it now, then maybe this will make you care."

His eyes narrowed. "What will make me care?"

She smiled and then aimed her wand at him. "Bye-bye."

With a slight *pop*, the branch beneath Elliot disappeared, and he found himself hurtling toward the ground. He knew he'd been high up before, but at the speed he was falling, the hard ground was only seconds away.

"Fid…get!" he yelled. "Help me!"

"Help yourself," she said, calmly flying beside him.

"What?"

"Just think about stopping, and you will."

"I can't!"

"Try it."

He flapped his arms and tried to think about stopping. But mostly all he could think about was panicking. And as everyone who has ever panicked before knows, it's not helpful for any kind of thinking.

Elliot looked down and saw the ground rushing up toward him. "Fidget! Help!"

"Think about stopping!" she insisted. "It's really important for you to do that. Right now!"

Elliot shut his eyes and whispered, "Stop, stop, stop," and then he yelled, "Stop!"

And everything stopped.

Elliot peeked with one eye, just to be sure he hadn't splattered onto the ground. Because if he had, he really didn't want to see what he looked like now.

Nope, he was still in one piece, and, oddly, he wasn't on the ground at all. Using both eyes now, he saw that the ground was in fact an inch or two below him. He had stopped in midair.

He blew out a heavy puff of air and landed on his face. Still lying flat on the ground, Elliot said, "Thank you, Fidget."

She landed gently on the ground beside him and sat on a small rock. "I didn't do that," she said. "You totally did it."

He lifted his head to look at her. A leaf was stuck to his forehead, but he left it there. "I did that? How?"

Fidget smiled. "Our gift to you is Pixie magic. You probably won't know how to use most of it, but you'll figure things out as you go. Totally awesome, right?"

"Totally." Elliot sat up and studied his hands. "I've got magic?" To test it, he raised his burned shoulder and thought the words, *Fix it.*

Answering his magical call, the threads of the shirt regained their color and wove themselves back together. The paste disappeared too, although Elliot noticed his skin was still a little green.

"Cool!" Elliot said.

"Lame," Fidget said. "I just gave you Pixie magic, and you use it to fix a shirt that doesn't even match my dress!"

"Okay. I can do better." Elliot stood and rubbed his hands together. Then he looked around for something bigger to test his magic on. He spotted Fidget's wand and wondered why she needed one and he didn't. Remembering the old cops-and-robbers games he used to play years ago, he closed one eye and pointed a finger at Fidget. "This is a stickup, so drop it!"

Just as he had hoped for, a spark of light shot from Elliot's finger and hit the wand, knocking it to the ground. But then a tall stick flew up from nearby and grabbed the back of Fidget's dress, carrying her high up into the air. Fidget screamed something about what she planned to do to him once she got down from there.

"Let her go, let her go!" Elliot cried. The stick immediately released her, and after a brief fall, Fidget's wings fluttered in the air. Her wand flew back into her hand, and she jetted angry sparks toward Elliot. He ducked, but the ends of his hair still got a little singed.

"That was so not awesome!" Fidget said. "What were you trying to do? Make me break a nail?"

"I thought it would only make you drop your wand," Elliot said. "I wondered if Pixie magic was strong enough to do that."

"Our magic isn't strong," Fidget said. "It's tricky. So be careful when using words like 'stickup.'"

"Sorry." Elliot scratched his head. "I bet it's strong enough for any reason I'd need it, though." It would've been cool to have this magic a year ago when Tubs Lawless was bullying him. But after Elliot won the Goblin war, he'd stood up to Tubs and hadn't been bullied since. Maybe he could ask Tubs to hit him one more time, just for the memories. Then *zapowie!* Pixie magic revenge!

Of course, with Elliot's luck, the Pixies would play a joke and take away his magic. Then it would just be *za-nothing* and a sore arm for Elliot where Tubs punched him.

"Our magic only helps you with tricks, not strength," Fidget said, still annoyed. "So stop playing around. It's time to fight Kovol."

"Can I fly?"

"We gave you magic, not wings."

Elliot didn't want wings anyway. He'd have to put holes in all of his shirts to fit them. Also, it would be hard to hide the wings from his mom. She would notice something like that.

"How do I poof?" Elliot asked. "I can do that, right?"

"Of course. That's like preschool magic. As clearly as you can, think of the place where you want to go, and then send yourself there." She tossed her hair behind her. "So where are we going?"

"*I'm* going home to check on my family," Elliot said. "*You're* going back to Burrowsville. I want everyone who can do battle to meet me in Demon Territory in one hour. Then we start to fight back."

For the first time, Fidget didn't seem to care how she looked or sounded. Her shoulders slumped and she said, "We gave you the best gift we could, Elliot. You have to help us win this war or everything will be destroyed."

Elliot smiled. "I will help. Totally."

Chapter 13

Where Kovol Knows Elliot's Name

Elliot's first ever experience of poofing himself somewhere wasn't as smooth as he had expected it to be. Finally he understood why the Brownies had so much difficulty poofing humans and why the Pixies made it such a rough trip. It was hard to take yourself out of one place and put yourself back together in another. There was a lot more to it than just thinking about where you wanted to go. The trip had happened in less than a second, and yet in some ways it felt more like an hour. At one point Elliot forgot to bring his feet along (and as you can probably understand, Dear Reader, his feet were very upset about being left behind—feet are picky about things like that), but when he opened his eyes, he was inside the bedroom of his house, feet and all.

The first thing Elliot did was to look under his pillow for Minthred's book. It was there, exactly as Fidget told him it would be. He retrieved it, then slid the book under his bed, far from where anyone might find it. Then he pulled off his shirt and shoved that under his bed too. He studied his green shoulder. The color had faded a little, but the burn seemed to have gone away. At least it didn't sting anymore.

He went to his closet for another shirt. The first one he reached for had a small ketchup stain on the sleeve. The second one was comfortable and in good condition, but it was a strange shade of blue. Fidget would say it didn't look like the sort of thing the leader of an Underworld war would wear.

"Argh!" Elliot said in frustration, then pulled the blue shirt from his closet. If he was going to fight an Underworld war, then he should at least be comfortable while doing it.

Next he went downstairs to find something to eat.

Wendy might not be the best cook ever, but he was pretty sure her food was better than whatever he might find in Demon Territory.

Or, wait—he had magical powers now. He could have any food he wanted. He could magic himself up a thick hamburger with all the toppings and a whole plate of fries. Or a big bowl of spaghetti. Or even a tray of doughnuts...with their holes. This magic thing was great!

"There you are," Wendy said when she saw him coming down the stairs. "I made you a sandwich an hour ago. It's been sitting for a while, so it's probably all dried out, but we can't waste the food."

Elliot's image of the doughnuts popped in his head like someone had put a pin to a balloon. He still wanted to use some magic to make himself lunch, but Wendy was sure to notice. He couldn't figure out any way to convince her that the doughnuts had just been left on the front porch by the mailman, or any other excuse.

Wendy was sitting on the couch still watching the news stories about the sinkholes. He grabbed the sandwich and took a bite, which promptly stuck in his throat. It took three swallows to get it down, and then it sat like a lump in his empty stomach. It was dry all right, like eating a piece of the Sahara Desert.

Dear Reader, if you are looking for a fun place to spend

your summer vacation, consider the Sahara Desert. It's as large as the entire United States, so you'll have plenty of room to play. Many different nomadic groups live there, so you're sure to meet lots of interesting people. And if you aren't attacked by sand vipers, scorpions, or the Saharan cheetah, you should be just fine. Unless there's a sandstorm. Or if you run out of water and can't find even one drop for hundreds of miles around you. Or if you forget to bring an extension cord long enough to charge your video game player. Also, you should know that you won't find many swimming pools in the Sahara Desert, so don't worry about packing a swimsuit. You won't need it.

While thinking of the hamburger he could be eating right now, Elliot choked down the rest of the Sahara Desert sandwich and then sat beside his sister.

She pointed to the television screen. "Look at this! Some new sinkholes started appearing on Main Street about ten minutes ago. Luckily nobody was hurt, but a lot of parked cars fell in."

Elliot looked around the room. "Where is everyone?"

"The twins went to make sure Uncle Rufus's jail hasn't sunk," Wendy said. Uncle Rufus had the unfortunate habit of stealing shiny things. Every time he got caught, he claimed he was too old to remember that it was still against the law to steal things. That trick had only worked the first ten times.

Elliot wished Wendy hadn't let the twins go, but at least the jail wasn't anywhere near Main Street.

"What about Reed?" he asked.

"He had to work at the Quack Shack," Wendy said. "I told him not to go, but Reed says he'll get fired if he doesn't have a good reason for not showing up."

"The Quack Shack is in the middle of all those sinkholes," Elliot said. "I think he has a really good reason not to go!"

"Reed didn't know about the holes when he left. But when they started happening, Cami said she'd go try to stop him. I'm sure they'll be back soon. Shh, the reporter's talking."

The cameras went live on Main Street, where the reporter explained that although most sinkholes are round, these new ones on Main Street had different shapes to them. "It's as if someone below the earth collapsed them to look just this way," he explained.

Then the camera cut to an overhead shot from a helicopter. At the angle the cameraman was shooting from, the shapes didn't appear to mean anything. The one at the top looked like a square *M*. Down from that shape were two sideways lines, and then there was a third, shorter line with a dot beside it. Next was a perfectly round hole, and finally, another sideways line at the bottom.

"What could these symbols mean?" the reporter asked. "Is it some message from aliens to Earth? A warning perhaps?"

"It's not aliens," Elliot mumbled. But it definitely was a warning.

"I guess we'll never know what it means," Wendy said. "I'll bet scientists will study this for years."

Elliot tilted his head to the side and looked at the Main Street sinkholes differently. "It's my name," he said. Looked at sideways, the square *M* was an *E*. The two lines were lowercase *L*s. Then the rest of the letters in his name followed.

Wendy laughed. "What? No." She tilted her head too, and said, "Your name has a *T* at the end. That last sinkhole shape just looks like another lowercase *L*. Your name isn't Elliol."

"I'm telling you, that's my name," Elliot said.

"You're being ridiculous!"

Then the camera shook and the reporter yelled, "It's happening again!" A puff of dirt rose in the air. When it cleared, the camera focused in on the newest sinkhole. Elliot sighed. Kovol had crossed the *T*.

"Oh, well, now I see your name," Wendy said. "That's weird."

"Not as weird as you might think," Elliot said. "I've got to go."

"Still working on that secret paper-mache project?"

"Huh?"

Wendy smiled. "You don't have to be embarrassed. Cami told us that you were working on a paper-mache doll of her and that you didn't want anyone to bother you in your room."

Elliot rolled his eyes. "That's what she said I was doing?" Couldn't she have picked something better? Like maybe he was lifting weights all morning or rescuing pets from burning houses? Then he sighed. A part of him wished Cami would have told Wendy the truth. It would have helped to talk to his sister about the Brownies and the Underworld war and about why there was a sinkhole on Main Street in the shape of his name. He was tired of keeping so many secrets from his family.

But it was not his secret to tell. The knowledge of the Underworld belonged to the creatures who lived there, not to him.

"Yeah, whatever Cami said, I have to go back and do that," Elliot said. "I'll be busy for a while, maybe a really long time."

"Okay." Wendy shrugged, then returned to watching the television.

Elliot ran back upstairs. As soon as he was out of sight, he closed his eyes, pictured the scene on Main Street, and poofed himself there.

Chapter 14

Where Kovol Wants a Duck Burger

Elliot might have thought about the shops and stores on Main Street, but he never could have pictured all the people running in the streets, pushing one another to get as far from the sinkholes as possible. He had tried to poof into a quiet part of the street, but when he got there it was obvious that nothing on this street was quiet today.

The sinkholes were in the middle of the road. From here, Elliot couldn't see his name, but he knew that hundreds of feet below this very spot, Kovol was sending Elliot the message that he was angry. Well, duh. Did he think Elliot hadn't figured that out yet?

"Excuse me," a woman said, nearly running him over.

He moved for her, which put him in the way of a man who only looked down at Elliot long enough to tell him to go home before he also hurried away.

Elliot wanted to get to the Quack Shack, but it was a little farther up the road. Elliot hoped Reed had seen the sinkholes and gotten away before he came into work. Elliot pushed past people who were pushing past him even harder. At first he had tried getting through politely by saying things like "Excuse me," or "Can I get by?" But now he just yelled "Move!" at anyone in his way.

"Elliot?"

He turned as Cami grabbed his arm. "I thought you were in the Underground," she said.

"The Underworld," he said. "I came back to check on my family."

"Thank goodness. Reed needs help."

"Reed? Where is he?"

For the first time ever, Elliot didn't care that Cami took his hand while she led him forward through the crowd. She was good at dodging people, and in no time they had made it to the front door of the Quack Shack. Through the main window they saw Reed on the floor, unconscious.

Elliot pushed on the door, but it wouldn't open.

"It's stuck," Cami said. "It jammed when the last sink-hole collapsed."

"Reed!" Elliot pounded on the window to wake up his brother, but Reed didn't move.

"We need to get some help." Cami stepped forward in the

crowd. "Excuse me, please—" But everyone passed her by, in their own hurry to leave Main Street.

While her head was turned, Elliot closed his eyes and pictured the door opening. He didn't think "un-jam" was a word, but he couldn't think of any other word to describe what he wanted the door to do. He whispered that to himself, then checked the door again. Something dark purple began oozing from the door near its handle. He leaned low and sniffed. It was sweet and fruity. On a guess, Elliot put a finger to the stuff and tasted it. Sure enough—grape jam! It was sort of gross, but the jam got into the lock and loosened the door enough for Elliot to inch it open.

"We're in," he called to Cami. "C'mon!"

She ran to help him with the door but then pulled her hand back. "Is that jam?"

"Don't ask," he said.

They rushed inside the Quack Shack and called again for help, but nobody answered. Reed was there alone, clearly because he was the only employee who thought the Quack Shack would be serving duck burgers while the entire city was collapsing.

Elliot dropped to his knees and shook his brother's arm. "Reed!"

Cami pressed her fingers to the side of Reed's neck to feel a pulse. "He's alive," she said. "But we've got to get him out of here."

"Help me lift him up." Elliot stood and tugged on Reed's arms, pulling him into a sitting position, and then saw two giant footprints in the floor beneath where Reed had lain. Not *on* the floor, but *in* it, smashed into the tiles.

"What could have done that?" Cami asked.

"Kovol," Elliot breathed. "Kovol was here. On the surface."

He quickly looked around them, then said to Cami, "I've got to try something that might feel weird to you. But you have to trust me, okay?"

She shrugged. "Okay. I trust you."

He put one hand on Reed's shoulder and took Cami's hand again. "It's better if you close your eyes," he said.

Elliot next closed his own eyes and pictured his bedroom as clearly as he possibly could. And poofed them all home.

It was harder than he had imagined. Instead of keeping one person's body parts together, now he had to do that for three people. And from the first second she had felt her gut being pulled away from the Quack Shack, Cami had started to do the girl-squeal thing. Even if poofing only lasts a single second, it can seem like hours if the girl next to you is squealing.

Then she stopped and they landed in Elliot's room. Somewhere during the trip, Reed had lost his Quack Shack apron, but Elliot hadn't worked very hard to keep track of that. All the important body parts seemed to have come back together and in their correct places.

"How did we get here?" Cami asked. "Did you do it?"

"I'm sort of new at magic, so I didn't do it very well." Elliot patted Reed's cheek. "Wake up. Please."

Slowly, Reed shook his head, then let out a long moan. His eyelids fluttered while he thought about waking up, and he raised a hand to his head.

"Ow," he mumbled.

"Are you okay?" Elliot asked.

Reed opened one eye and then the other. "Where are we?"

"Home."

"How did I get here?"

Cami began, "Elliot did some—"

"Really heavy lifting to get you here," Elliot finished.

"I had this horrible dream," Reed said. "I was in the Quack Shack, and this huge purple beast appeared. He asked if I was Penster. I said that I was Reed Penster and asked if he was hungry, because I figured even if he was a horrible beast, he'd probably order a lot of duck burgers. Then he roared and charged toward me. Then you appeared out of nowhere, Elliot, and dared the beast to come back and chase after you. He picked me up and threw me against the wall. The next thing I remember is waking up here."

Beside Elliot, Cami's mouth was hanging open almost to the floor. Elliot could only stare at Reed, relieved things hadn't been worse. Kovol must have lost Harold, who was shapeshifted as Elliot, so he came looking for Elliot in Sprite's Hollow. Luckily, Harold had arrived just in time to save Reed and got Kovol to chase after him again. But the chase could not last much longer. And Elliot could not let Kovol come back to the surface.

He quietly poofed the family's broom into his own closet, then stood and said to Cami, "Wendy will help you take care of Reed. And tell her to get the twins home and make them stay here."

"Where are you going?" she asked.

"You know where."

Then he grabbed the broom from his closet, walked into the hallway, and immediately poofed himself to the darkest part of the entire Underworld.

Chapter 15

Where Grissel Returns

Harold the Shapeshifter had been given only one job that day, which was to turn into Elliot and lead Kovol on a chase anywhere away from Demon Territory. Elliot hoped Harold had led Kovol and all of his army far away by now. Because if Harold made any mistakes, poofing into Demon Territory wasn't a good idea.

He was kidding himself, of course. It would *never* be a good idea to poof into Demon Territory.

But Elliot already had a plan

in mind. If Kovol was there, he'd just put up a magical shield or something. The only problem with this plan was that he had no idea how to create a magical shield, and he was pretty sure Kovol wouldn't give him any second chances to figure it out. So it wasn't a perfect plan.

It had been a bit of a trick for Elliot to poof himself into Demon Territory, because he had a hard time picturing exactly where he wanted to go. The only places he remembered there were dark enough to make him want to poof anywhere else. Finally he decided to go to the area right outside Kovol's cave. It was very dark there, but better there than inside the cave. On a scale of 1 to 10, with 10 being the creepiest place in the known universe, Elliot figured that spot was an easy 10. But it was way better than inside the cave, which was at least a 789.

Once he arrived, Elliot hunched down to the ground. He wasn't sure exactly why he did that, but it seemed like a good idea. Everything was as eerily quiet as it had been four months ago when he had first entered Demon Territory.

Not far from him was a puddle of mud with a brown glow around it. Elliot recognized it as gripping mud. He'd been stuck in it twice and had kept Kovol trapped in some until the solar eclipse earlier that day.

Elliot looked around carefully for any sign of smoke, which would indicate that the Shadow Men were nearby. But he saw nothing and hadn't really expected to. Kovol thought he was chasing Elliot across the Underworld, so he had likely called his army of Shadow Men to help him there.

Or most of his army anyway. There were thousands of Shadow Men. It wouldn't take long before some of them sensed that Elliot was in Demon Territory. If they told Kovol, he'd be all kinds of angry. Especially the bad kinds.

"Mr. Willimaker!" Elliot called.

Mr. Willimaker immediately appeared, holding his hands over his ears. "Your Highness, when you called just now, it was so loud, so different from before. How did you—"

"I've got magic," Elliot said, "from the Pixies."

"Ah. Well, then, you don't have to yell anymore to call us. We'll hear you fine." Mr. Willimaker pressed his thick eyebrows together. "Be careful about Pixie magic, Elliot. Like Pixies themselves, their magic will sometimes trick you."

Trick magic was still better than no magic, Elliot figured. But he only said, "I think so far we're alone here. When other creatures start appearing, I want us to use Kovol's cave as our defense. It's the closest thing Kovol has to a home, so I don't think he'd collapse it, even to fight us. I'll wait on top of his cave, watching for any sign of trouble. When everyone is ready down there, let me know. We're going to fight as many Shadow Men as we can before Kovol comes."

Mr. Willimaker bowed and poofed away. Then Elliot closed his eyes and poofed with the broom to the top of

Kovol's cave. It was higher off the ground than he had expected, but that only gave him a better view. Not that there was much to see. It was as black as midnight in all directions.

That didn't last for long, though. As the different creatures poofed into Demon Territory, they created enough light to help them see and to help Elliot see them. The Satyrs arrived first. They were as tall as the Elves, each of them with thick fur on the bottom half of their body, the hooves of goats, and a man's body on top. They had horns on their head and long ears that stuck out sideways. Then several Leprechauns flew in, each on the back of a Pegasus so white it almost created its own light. Elliot wasn't sure how he could use the Leprechauns (although he had plenty of ideas for how his family could use their gold), but he liked the flying horses. He wondered if the Underworld had any Dragons, because that would be cool too. Then he figured maybe it was better not to ask. Being creatures of fire, they probably had more in common with the Shadow Men than with him.

The Elves arrived next, and near the front of them was Slimmy Tojam. He nodded at Elliot, who only wanted to yell down to him that Minthred's book had been a huge waste of time. But if a goat herder could defeat Kovol, then surely Elliot could. He was only in fifth grade, but he was positive that was more education than Minthred had ever got.

He realized that several creatures hadn't come. Agatha wasn't there. There were several Fairies, but no Pixies. Many Brownies had come, but not the women or children, and Elliot was glad for that. He didn't want to risk anything happening to Patches.

Then Elliot saw Fudd poof in with a group of familiar creatures. The Goblins had arrived.

Elliot closed his eyes to poof himself down there. The Goblins looked surprised to see him use magic, but not Fudd, who obviously had not seen Elliot do anything at all.

"Well, well. Look at how the human king has grown," a voice sneered.

Behind all the other Goblins was Grissel. He was the strongest and boniest of all Goblins, and the meanest too. Every other Goblin was literally green with envy at the exact shade of Grissel's skin, for it was the closest in color to their favorite food, pickles. Grissel was plumper now than he used to be, due to the amount of chocolate cake he had eaten over his last several months inside Brownie jail. He was probably meaner too. "It looks like you've learned a few tricks since we last met," Grissel added.

When they had last met, Grissel and Elliot had tied in a battle to the death. It wasn't the first time they had fought. In fact, every time Elliot and Grissel met, it always seemed that Grissel was trying to finish him off.

"You'll fight for me?" Elliot asked Grissel.

Grissel's eyes narrowed. "I'll fight for the Underworld. I'll even fight for the Brownies, if necessary, to defeat Kovol. But I'd never fight for a human."

As if Elliot cared about a detail like that. "Then fight for the Underworld," he said. "I need the Goblins in front when the Shadow Men come. Slow them down by blowing things up. We can't fight all of them at once, but we can fight back if only a few get through at a time."

With that, Elliot turned to everyone else. He told his magic to make his voice louder, and when he spoke, it was as if he was speaking through a powerful microphone. "The Shadow Men are nothing but fire and darkness that Kovol has cursed. You can't fight them like a normal army, because they're not alive or dead. They're just a curse that will move until it's stopped. They will act like fire. If they surround you, they will suck air away from you. If they touch you, it will burn." Elliot looked over at Fudd. "And if they spit on you, it'll curse you too. But if you can suck the air away from them, you'll put out their fire. I bet it's the same if you get water on them."

"But how do we do that?" an Elf near Elliot said. "Only a few creatures have that power."

"It was a mistake to come," a Gnome grumbled. Several creatures muttered their agreement.

Elliot ran to a rock and stood higher up on it. He remembered his broom and held it up. "No, wait! If we try to fight this separately, then we will lose separately. The Underworld must stand together now."

"What's the broom for?" a Goblin asked. "Sweeping the Shadow Men out of here?"

"I can use this," Elliot said. "For when I fight the Shadow Men."

"What do you know about our fight?" a Centaur said. "You're not from our world."

"I'm not," Elliot agreed. "But I'm a part of it now. I always will be. I'll help save your world, and you'll help save mine. If you don't have power to control the air or water, then you still have something to offer. Light."

The creatures pressed closer, curious about Elliot's plan. He continued, "When the Shadow Men attacked Burrowsville earlier today, they couldn't push through the light. If they tried, they disappeared. So light is your weapon. Get a stick or a wand or whatever you have, and make it as light as you can. A Shadow Man is not only fire, he's also darkness. But your light is stronger than him. Dark cannot exist in light places. And we claim Demon Territory as a place of light now."

From his place on the rock, Elliot saw smoke in the distance, but coming closer. "They're early," he mumbled. He had hoped they wouldn't come so soon.

"Everyone find a place to hide," he called. "Goblins, you go to the border to slow them down. Get ready! The Shadow Men are here!"

Chapter 16

Where Harold Makes a Mistake

The battle of Demon Territory began with an explosion so big it rattled the entire ground. The wind it created rushed across the dark land, shaking the few trees and bushes that had dared to grow there.

Fudd stood on one side of Elliot and said, "That was Grissel. Nobody can blow things up the way he can." There was a hint of admiration in his voice, and even Elliot was impressed.

Elliot, Fudd, and Mr. Willimaker had returned to their places on top of Kovol's cave, but even from high up they couldn't see the Goblins.

The explosion created so much smoke near the border that it was impossible to see the difference between dust from the explosions and the Shadow Men moving deeper into Demon Territory. Elliot planned to keep everyone hidden for as long as possible. He didn't want the Shadow Men to have any warning in this battle.

But the Shadow Men must have already known something was wrong. Because as they flew close enough to be seen, their flight was swift and direct. They were coming to the cave and coming for a fight. If the heat of their black fire was any clue, this battle wouldn't be easy.

"Steady," Elliot whispered, more to himself than to anyone else. "Not yet. Not yet."

In the darkness, and with the speed of their flight, it was hard to tell how many were coming. Beside him, Elliot heard Mr. Willimaker trying to count them anyway. Fudd wiped sweat from his brow and looked nervous. Elliot wondered what it must feel like to sense the approach of the enemy but not be able to see them. Probably not great.

"How many do you think there are?" Elliot asked.

"At least fifty in the air." Then Mr. Willimaker pointed to the horizon. "And more are coming. Many more."

When the first of the Shadow Men was close enough that Elliot saw the fire in his cloak, he stood and yelled, "Underworld creatures, FIGHT!"

Immediately the territory came to life. The creatures focused any light they could into sticks, wands, and some even lit up their shoes for the fight. The Shadow Men swarmed in, and the battle began.

From where Elliot stood, he could see everything. The Brownies and Dwarves were doing their best with water. Their arms were too short to fight the Shadow Men alone, but the Brownies poofed in bucket after bucket of water for the Dwarves to throw on the Shadow Men, who quickly fell like drops of gray mud to the ground.

The Fairies and Pixies were working together to operate a giant fan that seemed to have the exact opposite effect of normal fans. Instead of blowing out cool air, it sucked in hot air. The Shadow Men who had ignored the fan at first were now too close and tried to fly away. But the fan continued pulling them in, and when it did, only ashes came out the other side.

Each Shadow Man destroyed took out another piece of Kovol's curse. Everything was going exactly the way Elliot had hoped it would.

The rest of Elliot's army fought one to one. They held off the remaining Shadow Men with their light sticks. None of the Shadow Men wanted to touch those sticks, which was fine with Elliot's creatures who really didn't want to get any closer than they had to.

In the distance, the Goblins continued to blow things up as new waves of Shadow Men approached. Every time Elliot heard an explosion, he knew that some had been slowed down and some had gotten through.

Yet so far, Elliot's side was holding its own.

"We're winning!" Elliot said excitedly to Fudd and Mr. Willimaker. "I think we're going to win this!"

Elliot may have spoken too soon. He heard a popping sound beside him and turned. In his human form, Harold was sitting beside Elliot, out of breath and with a very worried look on his face.

"I tried," Harold panted. "I tried, Elliot."

"Why are you here?" Elliot asked. "Where's Kovol?"

"I'm sorry. I made a mistake."

Elliot shook his head. "Harold, you were supposed to keep him far away from here!"

"I know." Harold took a deep breath. "I let him chase me everywhere. At one point he got bored and went up to the surface to look for you, but I got him back. But I got confused." Then his eyebrows pressed together. "I had to run so fast, and I forgot where I was. I led him back here."

Elliot gestured around them. "Here? You brought Kovol here?"

A deafening screech roared from the edge of Demon Territory. Hearing it, all the Shadow Men left Kovol's cave and flew away.

"That's Kovol calling his army back now," Harold said, burying his face in his hands. "We're in a lot of trouble, and it's all my fault."

Down on the dark ground, the Underworld creatures

looked around at one another, confused and alarmed. They had heard the screech too.

"What's happening?" a Centaur said. "Something's wrong."

"Everyone poof away from here!" Elliot cried. "Back to Burrowsville. Hurry!"

A few of the creatures obeyed, but most of them stared toward the border of Demon Territory, where smoke was gathering into the shape of a cone. It quickly twisted into a circle, slowly moving at the top, where it was widest, and spinning faster and tighter at the bottom.

"What is that?" Mr. Willimaker asked. "I've never seen anything like that before."

"We have those on the surface," Elliot said. "If that's what I think it is."

Elliot knew no one could stop what was coming. They weren't protected beside Kovol's cave. They were trapped there!

"That's a tornado!" he said. But unlike the tornadoes on the surface world, this one was made of smoke and fire. "Everyone hurry!" he yelled. "Poof out of here now!"

Chapter 17

Where Grissel Goes Free...Sort Of

"We have to leave now!" Fudd called to Elliot. Already, the wind created by the Shadow Men was so loud it sounded as if a train was running through Demon Territory.

Mr. Willimaker held tightly to his hat with one hand and to his glasses with the other. "It's too late," he said. "With wind this powerful, nobody could hold themselves together to safely poof away."

"Everyone go inside the

cave!" Elliot ordered. "There's less wind. You can poof away there!"

Nobody needed to be told. Creatures were already rushing into the cave. Above the noise of the wind, Elliot yelled to both Fudd and Mr. Willimaker to leave. They couldn't poof themselves, but Elliot helped them shimmy down the roof, then he used his broomstick to lower them into the arms of some nearby Trolls.

"You must come too," Fudd said.

"I'll wait until everyone else is safely inside, and then I'll come," Elliot said. Sure, that was the kind of thing a good leader did, but mostly Elliot still hadn't decided which was worse: Kovol's creepy cave or a huge tornado.

When the last of the creatures was inside, Elliot sat on the edge of the cave, preparing to jump to the ground.

Then suddenly he held his ears as a voice boomed inside his head. It was louder than the oncoming tornado and made his brain vibrate.

"Underworld creatures, you are in my territory, so you are my prisoners now!"

Elliot recognized Kovol's voice. Every word felt like fingernails scratching on a chalkboard.

But Kovol wasn't a ruler. Or was he? Could he order prisoners not to poof away? Elliot had been sure he couldn't, or else he wouldn't have brought everyone here.

Then Elliot asked himself why he had believed that Kovol couldn't take prisoners. Nobody had told him so. He hadn't asked anyone about it. Maybe he had convinced himself he was right because he wanted to be right, not because it was true. He had made a huge mistake!

"Nobody leaves this place," Kovol ordered. "I am coming! And I will destroy you all!"

When the voice had gone, Elliot slid the rest of the way down the cave and then ran inside. He tried not to look at the dark walls and wonder what crawled there. Or to peek in the direction where Kovol had slept for a thousand years.

The first thing he tried was to poof himself away. Maybe Kovol was wrong and couldn't make such an order. Or maybe this was like the movies. Since Kovol was the bad guy, then the good guys could find a way to ignore Kovol's order. But no matter how hard he concentrated on Burrowsville or his bedroom at home, or anywhere else, he couldn't leave. Along with every other creature still inside this cave, he was trapped.

"How many of us got away?" he asked. "Before Kovol made us prisoners."

Mr. Willimaker shrugged. "Not many. Maybe only a hundred or so. But hundreds more are still in here. There's nothing we can do but wait like trapped prey!"

"The Goblins are coming!" someone up front called. "Everyone scoot back, or we won't all fit!"

It was easy to smell when they entered. Elliot had thought the cave smelled bad before, but the Goblins brought it to a whole new level of stink.

"Where's Grissel?" Elliot asked a Goblin with a thin and bony face. But the Goblin shrugged and hurried away. So Elliot called out, "Does anyone know where Grissel is?"

Several of the Goblins pointed outside, and a tall one up front said, "The Shadow Men know that Grissel was blowing up Demon Territory. They have him trapped."

Elliot grabbed his broom and ran toward the mouth of Kovol's cave. He felt a tug on his arm and turned to see Mr. Willimaker with Fudd standing beside him.

"No, Your Highness. It's too dangerous," Mr. Willimaker said.

"Kovol will be here any moment," Fudd added. "You can't go out there."

Mr. Willimaker nodded in agreement. "Besides, think of everything that Grissel has done to you. He's not worth it."

Elliot said, "Every creature is worth it. I've got to help him." From here, Elliot felt a little of the wind created by the Shadow Men. It would be worse outside. He held his broom in front of him and thought the word "light," but when he peeked at the broom, it was only about as bright as a light bulb. That wasn't good enough. So he thought of the sunlight, of his family, and of everything good he had ever known, and he poured all of those thoughts into his broom.

Immediately the stick lit with a glow that spread light into every corner of the cave. Elliot held the broom high, then walked back into the storm.

There had to be hundreds of Shadow Men forming the tornado. It was taller than he could see and loud enough to make vibrations in his head. Somewhere in the middle of it all was Grissel. Elliot knew how it felt to be trapped as the Shadow Men sucked out all the air. He wouldn't let that happen to anyone, not even his Goblin enemy.

He tried pushing forward through the wind, but even with all of his concentration, there wasn't enough Pixie magic inside him to keep from being blown away. If he couldn't move forward, he couldn't save Grissel. The wind was so much stronger than he was. Then Elliot felt a sudden surge in his strength and slowly forced himself ahead. He took a quick glance behind him and saw many of the creatures at the entrance, their hands held out to him. It took a minute to understand what they were doing, and then he knew. He was moving forward by their power, not his own. They were using their magic to help him walk into a tornado.

When Elliot got close to it, he stretched out his arms with the lit broomstick. One by one, the Shadow Men crashed into the light, and one by one they fell to ashes. Elliot's arms shook from being so tired, but he held on. He *had* to hold on, because plan B (hoping the Shadow Men got dizzy and fell down on their own) was terrible. Gradually the wind died down as the Shadow Men either flew away or crashed into his broom and disappeared. He had fought a tornado and won!

When the last of them had gone, Elliot fell to the ground, exhausted. After only a minute he felt a bony hand on his arm, helping him to sit up.

"You're not such a bad human after all," Grissel said, smiling. "King Elliot, I promise never to harm your Brownies ever again."

"Then you're free to leave my jail," Elliot whispered.

"I don't think that matters," Grissel said. "You got rid of the Shadow Men for now. But all of us are trapped here in Demon Territory. And Kovol is coming."

Chapter 18

Where the Plan Fails

Elliot might have stopped the tornado of Shadow Men, but it didn't take them long to figure out where everyone was hiding. Elliot and Grissel had barely made it back into the cave before the Shadow Men returned.

"Quick!" Elliot said to the Goblins. "Blow up the entrance."

"But that will leave us trapped inside," an Elf said.

The Dwarves were the only ones who cheered at that idea. They often made their homes underground and, in fact, preferred living there. Everyone else started arguing.

"Better that we're trapped in here than to let the Shadow Men come and get us," Elliot said.

Grissel nodded his agreement with Elliot's order, and the Goblins raised their hands to blow up the cave entrance.

But it was too late.

Hundreds of Shadow Men flew inside the cave with so much speed, all that could be seen was their trail of black smoke, which quickly filled the air. Everyone began coughing and sputtering.

"Change into a stick," Elliot said to Harold between coughs. "Or a rock. Something that doesn't need to breathe."

"If it doesn't breathe, it doesn't think," Harold said. "I won't be able to think myself back."

"Do it!" Elliot said. There wasn't time for arguing.

He heard a small pop and saw a bright orange rock on the ground. "The idea was to be less obvious," Elliot muttered to Harold the Rock. Harold the Rock didn't answer. No big surprise. Rocks are not known for their skills at conversation. Even shapeshifted ones.

Elliot watched the remaining creatures try fighting back with their sticks of light, but without enough air they had no strength to hold on to them. The sticks lost their light and clattered to the ground. Even Elliot found he couldn't hold on to his broom. It was hard enough just to breathe.

One by one the dark claws of the Shadow Men reached out and touched several creatures on their heads. As they did, the creatures froze in place.

Elliot looked up from the ground where he sat, still coughing and choking on smoke. "What's happening to them?"

Beside him, Mr. Willimaker said, "They've turned to

stone. It's a curse. As long as the Shadow Men move, our friends will not."

Using the last bit of energy he had, Elliot wrote a message in the dirt. It said, "Orange rock."

Then as loudly as he could, he said, "The only one you want is me. If you leave these creatures alone, I'll let you take me to Kovol."

The Shadow Men stopped in midair. Only a few hundred creatures remained uncursed.

"No, Your Highness." Fudd stood and yelled to the Shadow Men, "Take me!"

"Or me!" Mr. Willimaker said.

They were joined in chorus by dozens of other creatures, each volunteering himself in place of Elliot.

Smoke instantly filled the room, making it even darker than pitch black. (Who knew that was even possible?) Elliot heard the thuds of bodies falling to the ground around him, and everything went silent. As the air gradually cleared, Elliot looked around the cave. Every other creature who had escaped being turned to stone had fallen on the ground. It looked like they were asleep, but they were moaning and shivering.

"What did you do?" Elliot yelled at the Shadow Men.

"A cold coma," the Shadow Men said in unison. "We pulled all the heat from their bodies."

"Well, give it back! I said I would go to Kovol *if* you left everyone alone."

Every Shadow Man in the cave, hundreds of them, laughed with one single laugh. Then together, all of them said, "Oh, but you will go to Kovol. He's ready for you now."

They began swirling around Elliot, choking off his air again. But this time there was no one to save him. His second-to-last thought was how tired he was of Kovol's army doing this, as if they didn't know any other tricks. It was like being a great pianist but knowing only one song. Elliot's last thought was that he was about to pass out, and that when he awoke again, he'd be facing Kovol as his prisoner.

Chapter 19

Where Elliot's Feet Complain

Oddly, when Elliot woke up, he was *not* facing Kovol, or even the Shadow Men. He was facing a tree, which as everyone knows is much less dangerous than an evil Demon and his army. He was also tied up and hanging upside down, which was a bigger problem. It was the sort of thing Tubs had done to him plenty of times. Elliot felt all the blood in his body rushing from his feet to his head, which he hoped would be a good thing. He figured since blood was important for living, it was probably just as important for thinking. And thinking was exactly what Elliot wanted to do right now. Besides, as long as he was tied up this way, he really had nothing better to do other than think.

As nice as the tree was to look at, Elliot twisted his body around to get a different view. He couldn't be certain, because things always look different when you're upside down, but he was pretty sure he was somewhere in the woods behind his house. Which meant Kovol was also here, or he would be soon.

Elliot thought about calling for help, but nobody would be this deep into the woods, especially not this late in the day. And he didn't know how he would explain what was happening, even if he did get someone to come.

Dear Reader, as one of the great coincidences of all time, the great adventurer Diffle McSnug was in these very woods only five minutes before Elliot arrived. Although Diffle has had many wonderful adventures, including his most recent trip down the rapids of the Nile River while balanced on a crocodile's back, Diffle has read the books of Elliot's earlier adventures and was very distressed to realize he was not a character anywhere in them!

So in the effort to make himself a character once and for all, Diffle came to the woods behind Elliot's house, sure that if he looked hard enough, he would find Elliot in great need of help. Once he rescued Elliot, he was sure to finally be made a character.

Unfortunately, Elliot was still in the Underworld at the time. Diffle forgot to look for him there, perhaps because he didn't know *how* to check the Underworld. Diffle can do many great things, but, alas, he cannot poof. Nor can he curl his tongue, but that's really not important right now. Diffle had left the woods only five minutes before Kovol brought Elliot here as his prisoner. Sadly, Elliot was, in fact, very much in need of help.

Since Diffle missed his chance to help Elliot, the decision by the Committee on Character Placement is that Diffle will not be admitted as a character in this or any other book about Elliot. After all his troubles, Diffle still needs to get his own book. Poor Diffle.

And poor Elliot! He just had to wait through an entire story about someone who isn't even a character in this book. Still upside down, and still all alone, with no chance for escape.

Or could he?

Because Elliot remembered he had Pixie magic. Most readers might think if they had Pixie magic, it wouldn't be the sort of thing they'd forget, whether they were hanging upside down or not. But Elliot had a good excuse. After all, he was facing the end of the world, which was partly his own fault since he did wake up Kovol. And if you recall, he'd only had the Sahara Desert sandwich for lunch, so he was also a little hungry. In other words, he'd had a hard day. Also, all the blood in his body was rushing to his head, so his thoughts were starting to get really crowded, and the thought about Pixie magic was stuck way in the back, where it had almost been forgotten.

With Pixie magic, escaping would be simple. All he had to do was poof away. Then maybe hide in the bushes until Kovol came and saw that his trap was empty. Elliot thought he'd love to see the expression on Kovol's face. He'd be so angry, he'd start ripping whole bushes right out of the ground…wait, now that Elliot had a chance to think about it, hiding in a bush was a terrible idea.

Elliot closed his eyes and told his body to poof out of the ropes. But nothing happened. He closed his eyes even tighter, and this time he ordered—no, he *demanded* that his body poof away. Again nothing happened.

"It's because I'm Kovol's prisoner," Elliot muttered. "Well, that's dumb."

But he wasn't finished yet. Maybe he couldn't poof away, but that didn't mean he had to stay here, tied up and helpless. He closed his eyes and imagined he was tied up with licorice ropes. Elliot planned to eat his way free—and get a yummy snack too! It was a perfect escape plan.

But as hard as he tried to make it happen, his ropes remained as they were, and Elliot remained stuck. However, he was able to poof in a piece of licorice to snack on while he thought of a new plan. So his Pixie magic wasn't completely useless.

Then Elliot's eyes widened. He might be trapped here, unable to use magic to free himself, but there were still things he could do.

"Patches!" he hissed. "Patches, I need you!"

Instantly, Patches appeared and hugged his face, the only part of him she could reach. "There you are! Kovol must have found some way to block us from finding you." She frowned. "Are you okay? Your face is really red."

"All my blood is in my head right now. But that's okay. It's helping me think...or I think it's helping me think."

With a shrug, she said, "If you say so. And where's everyone else? They haven't come back from Demon Territory yet. The creatures who stayed behind are getting worried."

"That's why I need your help. I need you to find Agatha the Hag. Most of the creatures who were fighting with me in Demon Territory are in Kovol's cave. Agatha's the only one I know with a light bright enough to hold off the Shadow Men, if they're still there." He didn't want to tell Patches how the Shadow Men had left most of the creatures as stone statues, and others, like her father, in cold comas. Or that the creatures were all Kovol's prisoners now and couldn't escape, even if Agatha was somehow able to heal them. But he had left Agatha the note in the dirt to look for the orange rock. She would know what to do. Elliot looked back to Patches. "Ask Agatha if she'll go to that cave and see if she can help."

"Okay, but what about you?" Patches asked.

"Can you cut me down?"

"Not while you're Kovol's prisoner," she said. "But when I come back, I'll help you fight him."

"No, don't come back," Elliot said. "I'll figure things out here on my own."

As soon as Patches was gone, Elliot looked around the area, trying to figure out other ways to use his magic against Kovol. He couldn't think of any decent ideas. Even if he did know a good trick, there was always the chance that it would backfire and make things worse.

Maybe Elliot had been wrong about all the blood in his head helping him think. Thinking was actually getting pretty hard. Also, his feet were beginning to complain about not getting their fair share of blood.

Only one thought had worked its way through Elliot's brain, the one idea that might be the perfect trick against Kovol. Elliot twisted around until he found the exact spot he was looking for, then closed his eyes and made his idea happen. There was no way to tell if it would work. And it wouldn't do him much good unless he was able to get out of this rope.

He squirmed and kicked and tried to think himself thinner. But none of it worked.

Being Kovol's prisoner was starting to get old.

Chapter
20

Where Kovol Needs Deodorant

When Kovol finally returned for Elliot, he seemed to be in a worse mood than usual. At least he snorted a lot, and stomped his feet, and had this low growl that wasn't too different from the way Reed sounded on days he had to wake up extra early for school. It was no surprise to Elliot that Kovol was in a bad mood. Ever since he'd become king, Elliot had noticed that bad moods were normal for evil creatures. And if they were in good moods, it was probably because one of their evil plans was going well. So the bad mood didn't bother Elliot nearly as much as a good mood would.

"It sounds like destroying Earth is a lot tougher than you thought it would be," Elliot said. He figured that he and Kovol might as well have some conversation.

But Kovol only grunted. He paced back and forth, every so often looking up at the bright springtime sky. Maybe he was waiting for the sun to go down before he did anything really mean. Elliot understood that. He had always felt that if he were a super villain, he'd do all of his super-villain work at night too—as long as he had taken a nap in the daytime so that he didn't get tired.

Elliot wondered if Kovol had taken a nap that day. Probably not. He'd probably had more than enough naptime in the last thousand years.

"I have a question," Elliot said. "What are you planning to do after you destroy Earth? Because if you destroy my world, then you destroy yours too. What if you get bored and want some candy from the store? But there is no store because you destroyed it?" Elliot shrugged. "I'm not sure that you really thought this plan through."

"I will destroy Elliot," Kovol muttered.

"Well, yeah, I think you've made that clear," Elliot said. "But what about everything else? Maybe you haven't noticed, but Demon Territory is the ugliest, stinkiest, dirtiest place in the entire Underworld. And if you go around destroying all the nice places, you'll be stuck without a home."

"I'll destroy everything," Kovol said. "Except for one sunny island."

Elliot's ears perked up (except he was still upside down in

the rope, so his ears actually perked down). "Oh, like Fiji or somewhere? My teacher went there for a trip last year."

Kovol grunted, which was probably a yes.

It gave Elliot another idea. Hiding his grin, he said, "So you don't want to destroy *everything*. Mostly just me, right?"

Again, Kovol grunted a yes.

"What about all those creatures you took prisoner inside your cave? Are you going to destroy them?"

This time Kovol spoke in sentences. "I'll rule those who serve me. Those who fight me get eaten."

Elliot thought that was a pretty lame way to rule. The Brownies didn't bow to Elliot because otherwise he would eat them. They bowed because he served them and loved them and did everything he could to make their lives better.

But to Kovol he only said, "I'm the one who got all those creatures to fight you. I'm responsible for that."

"So I must destroy Elliot," Kovol grunted again.

"Yes, I *know*. But you've already got me. So it doesn't make sense to keep all those other creatures as your prisoners."

"You're right," Kovol agreed. "I need creatures to serve me."

"So you wouldn't care if everyone you took prisoner down there went free?"

"No."

Elliot hoped that would be enough. He wasn't clear on how all the rules of magic worked, but Kovol had just said he didn't care if all the creatures he had taken prisoner went free. Was that enough to release them?

Technically speaking, Elliot was also one of the creatures that Kovol had taken prisoner. So if they were free, did that mean Elliot was free too?

There was only one way to find out. Elliot closed his eyes and tried to think of a place where he wanted to poof himself. But it wasn't an easy decision. Wherever he went, there was a chance that Kovol might follow. So he couldn't go home or to Burrowsville. And he didn't want to go to Demon Territory, where Kovol could take him prisoner again. If he got the chance, he wouldn't mind stopping the war long enough for a bathroom break. That would give him a good place to think.

Elliot was usually a pretty good thinker. But sometimes he was also a pretty slow thinker, and trying to figure out where to poof was definitely *not* a good time for him to take so long to think.

Because while Elliot's eyes were shut, Kovol decided he might as well just get rid of his prisoner once and for all. He made a twirling motion with his fingers, and Elliot started spinning with his rope. "I like my breakfast scrambled," Kovol said.

"News flash," Elliot called back. "Breakfast was hours ago! I guess you'll have to wait until morning." Except he already felt his insides scrambling. He didn't want to do this all night.

Elliot opened his eyes only long enough to figure out that he was getting dizzy really fast. Then he closed them again and tried to poof away to anywhere. It didn't matter. He'd poof to the top of Mount Everest if he had to. Or to the moon. Or, better yet, to Fiji. He thought Fiji might be nice this time of year.

But with so much blood crowding out the other thoughts in his head, and with the problem that he was now spinning like a top, Elliot couldn't form a single picture of anywhere he ought to go. In fact, he couldn't put any thought together that made sense. He started sputtering things back to Kovol like "I…you…sometimes pickles…let's dance."

He wasn't sure what that meant. Kovol didn't seem to understand it either, because he slowed Elliot's spinning long enough to say, "No more. With Elliot gone, no one rules the Underworld but Kovol!"

Kovol raised his arms above his head to strike at Elliot, releasing the most horrible armpit odor that had ever been sent into the world. A butterfly that had just flown into the area exploded as soon as it crossed the smelly vapor. When the breeze carried the odor to a fat pine tree, eight of its branches fell straight to the ground. If Kovol's armpits had smelled good, like a fresh-baked apple pie or something, Elliot still would have wanted to live. But to have that disgusting stench be the last thing he ever smelled—he could not accept that!

So he closed his eyes and made the decision just to poof out of the rope, where Kovol was aiming his curse. He wasn't sure where he'd go next, but all he cared about was getting away from that smell.

While Elliot was thinking, Kovol began building his magic. The skin on Elliot's arms prickled with static as the magic gathered between Kovol's beefy palms. It felt like a ball of invisible lightning, and when it was all gathered, Elliot knew it was coming straight for him. This was exactly what Fudd had warned him about earlier that day.

"Poof!" he ordered whatever part of his body controlled the magic. But he felt nervous about what Kovol was doing, and it was hard to concentrate, even to drop out of the rope. Elliot realized he didn't know for sure that he *could* poof away. Maybe his trick to have Kovol release all the prisoners had worked. And maybe not.

"Poof!" he said aloud. He closed his eyes and pictured himself falling onto a soft mattress pad right below him.

But the magic failed again, and whatever Kovol held between his palms was beginning to spark.

"This is the end!" Kovol said. "Now I destroy you."

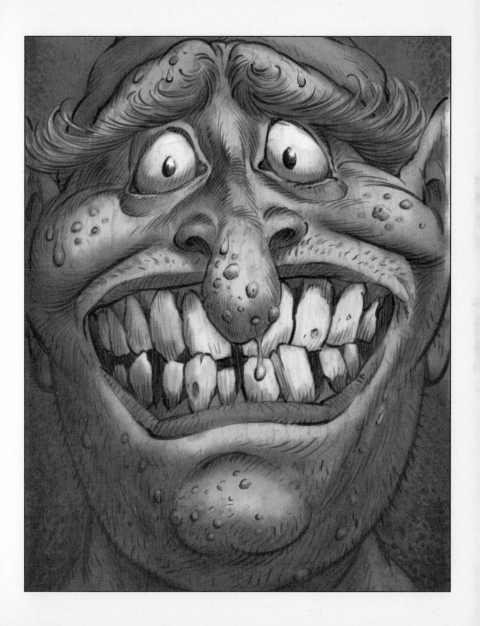

Chapter 21

Where Grissel Bows

Despite what Kovol had threatened, it wasn't the end, or at least not the end of Elliot. Because with a very loud yelp, Kovol was suddenly thrown into the air as the ground beneath him exploded. Kovol was many things—all of them bad—and this included how bad he was at flying. Kovol shot high into the air, his arms flailing and his roar echoing higher and higher into the air.

"Poof!" Elliot said again. And this time the magic worked and Elliot fell onto the ground. Unfortunately, he had forgotten to include the soft mattress this time, so his fall kind of hurt. But not as much as a ball of lightning would have, so he didn't complain.

He sat up but remained on the ground for a moment while all the blood in his body went back to where it was supposed to go. He ran his fingers through his hair and tried to figure out what might have caused that explosion. He knew only one creature who could do something like that.

"We're even now," a voice behind Elliot said.

Elliot turned, surprised to find that he was actually pleased to see Grissel standing there. Grissel had hated Elliot from the moment he heard about him on a Halloween night more than three years ago. He had tried to destroy Elliot ever since Elliot became king of the Brownies, and had refused to stop trying, even if it meant suffering the cruelest ever punishment of nothing to eat but chocolate cake…without frosting! And yet Elliot had saved his life. Now Grissel had come to repay the favor.

"How did you get here?" Elliot asked. "I thought the Shadow Men turned everyone into stone or put them in cold comas."

Grissel shrugged. "Agatha found the orange rock that was your Shapeshifter. She helped him change back, and then he explained what had happened. When the Hag transforms, she isn't nearly as pretty to a Goblin's eyes, but her light is very warm. With that light, she can heal the curse of the cold comas. She healed me first and is still healing the others."

"What about those who were turned to stone?"

Grissel shook his head. "They cannot be healed as long as the Shadow Men fly."

"Then I need you to go back and protect them," Elliot said.

"Until I find a way to stop the Shadow Men, I don't want anything else to happen to our friends."

Grissel blinked at Elliot. The corners of his mouth began to splinter as if he was trying to make an expression that his face was not used to. After some serious cracks, his mouth formed something that almost looked like a smile. Then he bowed and said, "King Elliot, many of those stone creatures are my friends too. I didn't think you would care about us, but I was wrong. I will not allow harm to come to anyone in the cave until you find a way to save them."

"Thank you, Grissel," Elliot said.

"No, King Elliot," Grissel said. "Thank *you*." After a short bow, Grissel disappeared.

Elliot waited only a moment before calling for Harold. He didn't know how far away the explosion had carried Kovol, but they didn't have much time. He waited a moment, sure that the Shapeshifter must not have heard him. Then he yelled, "Harold!" again.

He had expected to see Harold arrive in his human form, but instead a mosquito popped onto Elliot's nose. If Elliot could have seen it with a magnifying glass, he would have noticed the small white patch of hair on the mosquito's head—a sign that this was his friend. But Harold the Mosquito only buzzed, "No! Leave me alone!" Then he gave Elliot a bite, because that's what mosquitoes do. And he poofed away.

Elliot itched his nose, then said, "Harold, get back here right now! I have to talk to you!"

A small spider monkey appeared in the tree above Elliot. Same white patch of hair, same Shapeshifter. "No!" the monkey howled. It looked around for a bunch of bananas, but since this was not a banana tree, it threw some pinecones at Elliot's head and poofed away again.

Elliot stood up and put his fists on his hips. "Harold! You will come here right now, or I will tell Cami that we never want to see her again."

Several seconds passed when Elliot thought even that threat wouldn't be enough to bring Harold back. Finally he poofed in front of Elliot, in his human form. But his arms were folded, and the look on his face was somewhere between upset and furious.

"Don't ask me for anything else, because I won't do it," Harold said. "You gave me one job, to keep Kovol away from Demon Territory. I didn't do that right. And then down in Kovol's cave, I should have transformed into a Hag and tried to put off enough light to chase the Shadow Men away, but I didn't do that either. All I did was turn into an orange rock. Not diamond or gold or some useful metal. Just a dumb orange rock. I don't dare to do anything else to help. I might be more dangerous to our side than Kovol."

Truthfully, that same thought had occurred to Elliot. But

he hoped this time he had found something so harmless that even Harold couldn't ruin it. Elliot sighed as he stared at his friend. Who was he kidding? Nothing was too harmless to be safe from Harold.

"Just come with me, please," Elliot said, and then quickly added, "And before you tell me no again, it's something with Cami."

Harold's eyebrows lifted. "Cami?"

Elliot smiled. "Cami with Warts—I mean, Cami Wortson, the love of your life."

"I'd do anything for the love of my life," Harold said. "You know I would. But I can't risk making any more mistakes."

"Are you kidding?" Elliot said. "Do you know how many mistakes I've made since becoming king? Maybe you made a mistake by bringing Kovol back to Demon Territory, but it was really my mistake for having us go in there unprepared. Everyone makes mistakes. But my dad says that's always okay, *if* you're willing to fix them."

Harold sighed. "How do I fix this?"

"Let's go back to my house," Elliot said. "We'll poof straight to my room."

"Okay," Harold said glumly. "I just hope you know what you're doing letting me make mistakes around your family."

"Uh—" Elliot began. But it was already too late. Harold had poofed away.

Chapter 22

Where Harold Confesses

When Elliot and Harold poofed into Elliot's bedroom, they found Cami on the floor reading a book. She jumped to her feet, startled. "Oh, you scared me!" Once her heartbeat started up again, she said, "I'll never get used to you doing that."

"I'll never get used to doing it either," Elliot said, although he had already begun to think that magic might be the perfect solution to his problem of getting to school on time. He added, "How's Reed?"

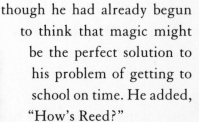

"He still thinks it was all a dream," Cami said.

"After he rested for a while he felt better, but he's definitely not going back to the Quack Shack today."

Elliot hoped the Quack Shack would still exist after today. Not only because it would mean Kovol had failed in destroying the world, but also because he really liked duck burgers.

"Are there any new sinkholes?" Elliot asked.

Cami shrugged. "The reporter who was covering the story fell into one and broke his leg. They can't do any more news on the sinkholes until they find another reporter who'll agree to go out there." Then she noticed Harold, who had done nothing but stare lovingly at her since he poofed in. "Who's this? Another king?"

Harold fell to his knees in front of her. "Do you know how wonderful it is to look at you through my own eyes? How do I describe the joy of looking at you looking at me as I look back at you?"

Cami made a face and turned to Elliot. "What's he talking about?"

"Get up, Harold." With his foot, Elliot nudged the Shapeshifter in the back.

Harold started to stand up, but Cami put a hand on his shoulder and pushed him down again. "Wait a minute." She fingered the patch of white hair on Harold's head. "I've seen this before."

Harold froze, looking as guilty as if he had just been

caught robbing a bank. Elliot shook his head, mad at himself for forgetting that Cami was actually a pretty smart girl.

Her eyes narrowed as she first stared at Elliot. "About four months ago, I saw this exact patch of white hair on your head for a few days. And for those days, you were acting so strangely. Sort of like—" Now she turned to Harold. "Sort of like *you* were acting just now!"

Elliot tried to look innocent. "Hmm, that's weird."

But Harold cried out, "I can't lie to the love of my life!" Now he stood, but he clasped his hands as he faced Cami. "Elliot was trapped in the Underworld, and he begged me to come up to the surface and pretend to be him."

Elliot's nose wrinkled. That wasn't the way he remembered it, although he was certain that was exactly the way Harold did.

"But how could you do all that?" Cami asked. "You don't look anything like Elliot."

Harold blew out a deep breath, and as he did, the bones and coloring of his face shifted to match Elliot's. Other than the white patch, his hair lightened to dark blond, and even his clothes changed to a simple T-shirt and jeans, exactly the same as Elliot's.

Cami let out a scream. Not a big scream or a long scream, but a very girly scream that made Elliot's toes curl.

"Change back!" he said to Harold. "Hurry!"

"Yes," Cami agreed. "This is so creepy!"

With another deep breath, Harold returned to his usual form. He said nothing more, but his eyes pled with Cami to accept him for who he was, in whatever form he might happen to be.

"You can change shapes?" she asked.

"He's a Shapeshifter," Elliot said.

"And what does he really look like?"

Elliot shrugged. "Whatever he wants."

Cami looked from Elliot to Harold and back to Elliot, and with each turn of her head, her face got redder and redder.

"Are you mad?" Elliot asked. Was it really such a big deal if a Shapeshifter had pretended to be him for a few days? So what if the only reason he and Cami were sort of friends was because Harold had been so nice to her during that time? He really didn't see what the problem was.

Cami poked Elliot in the chest. "I decided to be friends with you because you were so nice when we did the science experiment together. But that wasn't you being nice. It was him. Which means you never wanted to be my friend in the first place!"

Elliot wanted to tell her she was wrong about all of that, but she wasn't. It had never been his idea to be Cami's friend. However, now that she was, he didn't mind it so much. In fact, sometimes her friendship wasn't awful at all.

Then she turned to Harold. "Why do you keep saying I'm the love of your life?"

He smiled shyly. "Because you are the most wonderful human I've ever known. The most beautiful, the kindest, and with a voice that melts my heart."

Elliot couldn't stop himself. He gagged.

Cami's face scrunched up. "Get out!" she said to Elliot.

Elliot backed up a step. "It's my room!"

"I don't care. Get out!" Turning to Harold, she added, "If you really liked me, then you wouldn't have lied about who you are! You get out too!"

She backed both Elliot and Harold out of his room, then slammed the door on them. The door even flattened Harold's nose for a second before it popped back into place.

"Quiet up there!" Wendy hissed from downstairs. "Reed's asleep."

Harold turned to Elliot, his eyes wide. "The love of my life yelled at me."

"I guess we probably deserved it," Elliot said. "I never thought of how she'd feel about you pretending to be me."

Then Harold smiled. "Hey, I just realized that was our first fight. One day she and I will look back on this moment and laugh about it all."

Elliot rolled his eyes, then cracked open the door to his room. Cami still stood in the doorway with her arms crossed and eyebrows pressed low. Before she could speak, he said, "We're both sorry about what we did. And it's okay if you don't want to forgive us yet, but we really need your help."

"How?"

"Do you still have the paper-mache doll of me from when we played Capture the Flag this morning?"

"You made fun of it."

"I know. I'm sorry about that too. But I need it now."

"I already took the doll home."

"Can you go get it? And then maybe bring it to the same place in the woods where you had it this morning?" She hesitated, and he added, "You don't have to do this for me, or for Harold, but would you do it for the human race?"

Slowly, Cami nodded. "I'll do it for the human race, minus you two."

Harold smiled. "Actually, I'm not part of the human race. I'm just in that form right now."

Cami's face reddened again, but Elliot took another step forward and said, "No, that's good. Stop talking, Harold." Then he called, "Patches! I need some turnip juice." While he waited for her to come, he asked, "Are the twins home now?"

"They got home about ten minutes ago," Cami said. "Wendy's feeding them some dinner. She offered me some too, but I'm not sure it was food."

Whatever it was, as long as it could be eaten, it sounded good to Elliot. But he didn't have time to eat now.

Patches poofed in with a large bottle of turnip juice in her hands. "Here it is. Are you thirsty?"

"Not exactly." Elliot looked at Harold. "Now can you turn into a goat?"

Harold winked at Cami. "Goats are one of my better animals. I know you'll be impressed."

From the little that Elliot knew about girls, he guessed Cami wasn't likely to be impressed with Harold's changing into any farm animal. Except maybe a horse. He knew most girls liked horses.

Harold let out a deep breath, and his body immediately curved so that he stood on four hooves rather than hands and feet. White hair spread all over his body, and his face molded into that of a goat's.

"Ho-oww do you like me no-oww?" he asked Cami.

"Eww," Cami said.

Then he bleated to Elliot, "Wh-y do you ne-eed a goat?"

Elliot took the bottle from Patches and held it out to Harold. "Spit in this," he said. He wasn't sure whether Minthred's sleep recipe would work, but it was worth a try.

Harold the Goat gathered a big wad of spit in his mouth, then shot it into the bottle.

"Disgusting!" Patches cried. "No Brownie will drink that now."

"I don't want a Brownie to drink it," Elliot said, putting

the lid on it again. "I have much bigger plans for this. There's just one more ingredient I need. Anyone know where I can get some earwax?"

Everyone in the room stared at one another, but no one seemed to have any earwax available at that moment.

"Can you get some here by magic?" Cami asked.

"Magic can't just create something from nowhere," Patches explained. "It has to exist somewhere first."

"We need to think of someone who would have a lot of earwax," Harold said, tapping his hoof on the floor.

"The Trolls?" Elliot suggested. "I've seen their ears, and there's got to be pounds of it in their heads."

"But Agatha told me they're all turned to stone," Patches said. "If we got any, it would be stone earwax."

They all froze when a roar boomed from the woods behind Elliot's house, rattling the windows and even shaking a few books from Elliot's bookshelf.

"What was that?" Cami whispered.

"Kovol," Elliot breathed. Kovol was looking for him.

"You've got to poof somewhere far away," Patches said. "Where Kovol won't think of looking for you."

"I can't," Elliot said. "When he couldn't find me before, he went after Reed. I have to go back and face him now, or he'll look for my family. Harold, will you stay here as me to protect them, just in case?"

"What if I mess up?" Harold asked.

"You won't," Elliot said. "I know this time you won't."

"What can I do?" Cami asked. "I promised you I'd help."

"This is my fight," Elliot said. "Just get that paper-mache doll into the woods." He pointed to the jar of turnip juice and goat spit. "Keep track of this too. It's really important now."

"It's also really gross now," Patches said. Then she added, "Be safe, Elliot."

Before Kovol had finished his second roar, Elliot closed his eyes, pictured Kovol so clearly it made his knees turn to rubber, and then poofed himself there, ready for the final battle.

Chapter 23

Where the Magic Fails

Sometime last year Elliot had seen a cartoon about a kid who battled hundreds of alien invaders all by himself to save planet Earth. He had liked the movie, but that's all it was, just a story a bunch of writers had made up. Right before poofing back to the woods to face Kovol, Elliot tried to think of even one true story where a kid does battle with someone a lot stronger and wins.

He didn't know any. Not even one.

But he couldn't worry about that with Kovol. Besides, Elliot liked the idea of being the first kid ever to win against such odds. Of course, he wouldn't be able to tell everyone that he was the one who saved Earth. Maybe when he was a hundred years old and on his deathbed, he could gather his friends and family around him and say, "Did I ever tell you about the time I saved the world?" Yeah, that'd be cool. He was going to put that on his calendar for eighty-nine years from now. *If* he was still alive eighty-nine minutes from now, of course.

Elliot's plan had been to poof in quietly and make the first attack on Kovol. And it would have been a fine plan, except he maybe did too good a job in picturing Kovol and poofed in right on top of the evil Demon's head. Since Kovol was bald, Elliot slipped off his head and would have fallen all the way to the ground if he had not grabbed on to each of Kovol's long, twisted horns.

Kovol yelled and swung his head, trying to get Elliot off. Elliot would have been very happy to get off, but he couldn't let go with Kovol swinging him so hard. His body was flung around wildly in the air. Kovol got angrier and angrier, twisting his head as far to the right as he could. Elliot's body flew all the way around Kovol's head, and he accidentally kicked Kovol in the nose.

Kovol fell back in pain, and this time Elliot let go of the horns and scrambled free as fast as he could.

"So that's how you want things to be," Kovol muttered.

No. Actually, the way Elliot wanted things was for Kovol to never have woken up in the first place. Or if he did wake up, he'd have wanted Kovol not to have made such a big deal about Elliot's taking his last hair. Maybe Elliot could have politely apologized for taking the hair, and then Kovol would've said, "That's okay," and they could've played a game of Limburger soccer instead of all this.

However, none of that was going to happen.

Kovol charged for Elliot, with his bruised nose snorting and his claws out. Elliot whispered to his magic, "Block him," fully expecting a shield to come up between them. But instead, a pile of toy building blocks fell from nowhere above them, landing on Kovol like a perfectly square hailstorm. Kovol looked up to see what was happening, and the corner of a block landed straight in his eye.

"Ow, my eye!" Kovol yelped. "Why would you do that?"

Stubbornly, Elliot folded his arms. The blocks had been an accident, but this was supposed to be an ultimate battle to save the world, so he wouldn't apologize.

"That's right." Elliot tried sounding as tough as he could. "And there's more where that came from!"

Maybe that was true, maybe not. He wasn't really clear on where any of this was coming from.

Kovol huffed and ran toward Elliot again. But Elliot was getting the feel of Pixie magic now. It wasn't great magic for strength or power, but it was excellent if you were trying to trick someone.

So when Kovol started running, Elliot pictured old-fashioned roller skates on the bottom of the Demon's feet. To make it funnier, he pictured girly ones. Even pinker than a Pixie dress and with glittery hearts covering every inch of them.

The skates appeared, and with his arms flailing around, Kovol rolled right past Elliot and crashed into the trunk of a wide oak tree. Even though he knew he shouldn't, Elliot laughed. Besides, why not? Kovol's anger couldn't get any worse. He hoped.

If Kovol had been a Troll or even a Goblin, Elliot probably could have continued with magical jokes for the rest of the day. But Kovol couldn't be tricked for long. And he definitely didn't think the roller skates were nearly as funny as Elliot did. Once he kicked them off his feet, he turned and hurled back a ball of energy so fast that it threw Elliot into the air. Elliot landed with a hard thump on the ground.

Now it was Kovol's turn to laugh. Only, unlike Elliot's happy laugh over a funny joke, his was dark and mean and made Elliot think maybe he didn't want to get back up again.

Still seated, Elliot tried throwing an energy ball of his own at Kovol, but it came out more like a gentle puff of air. Kovol swatted it out of the way like he would a bothersome fly.

"Pixie magic," Elliot whispered. It wasn't about strength. It was about trickery. He had the idea to make it rain actual cats and dogs, but Kovol struck at him first, creating a sinkhole exactly where Elliot was sitting. With nothing but air suddenly beneath him, Elliot fell. He tumbled head over heels into a hole that looked bottomless. Finally he found the magic to grab on to a dangling tree root, and then he began the long climb back to the surface. Kovol stood at the top of the sinkhole with his smelly armpits raised again. He was gathering more lightning between his clawlike hands.

"Oh, no you don't!" Elliot closed his eyes to picture the edge of the sinkhole becoming a sheet of thick ice. Kovol slipped on the ice that magically formed and landed on his large Demon backside, then slid over the edge and right past Elliot into the sinkhole.

"Gotcha!" Elliot called. Then he poofed back to the surface and brushed his hands together. Carefully he peered over the edge, curious about how far into the hole Kovol had fallen.

But Kovol wasn't down there. Which means he had—

"No, I've got *you*!" From behind, Kovol grabbed Elliot around the waist and lifted him into the air.

Elliot put his hands over Kovol's and tried to pry himself free, but Kovol was a lot stronger than Elliot, even with the Pixie magic.

"I'll take your magic before eating you," Kovol said. "You'll taste better that way."

"I'll taste terrible!" Elliot said. "I haven't had a bath for three days!" He couldn't let Kovol take his magic. For that matter, he really didn't want to be eaten either.

Elliot squirmed, but it was useless. He tried to pull

together enough magic to get away from Kovol, but he was being squished too tightly for the magic to work properly. Elliot felt a little frustrated by that. If he had invented magic, he would have made it so you could use it even when you were squished. Or maybe *especially* when you were squished.

Kovol pulled him back over solid ground. Elliot knew for a fact that it was solid, because Kovol dropped him on it. He tried rolling away so that he could gather some magic to defend himself, but Kovol immediately put a foot on Elliot's chest. That made it hard to do magic, which was a problem. It was even harder to breathe, which was a much bigger problem.

Standing over him now, Kovol started moving his arms, almost as if he were pulling an invisible rope out of Elliot's body. Elliot felt the magic being dragged out of him, and he held on to it with all of his strength. But strength was not one of the gifts of Pixie magic, so all Elliot had was his own determination not to let Kovol take this magic. It would only make Kovol more powerful, and it would leave Elliot completely defenseless.

Elliot swatted at the Demon's foot with his hands, but it didn't do any good and only tired him out faster. He closed his eyes, searching for enough magic left inside him to fight back. Anything. But as hard as he searched, he found nothing at all. If he couldn't figure out something soon, the last Underworld war would be over in the next few minutes.

Chapter 24

Where Tubs Teaches Kovol

Just when Elliot thought he could hold on no longer, he heard a voice somewhere in the woods behind him. "Let go of our brother!"

"No!" Elliot cried in the loudest voice he had (which at that point was little more than a whisper). That was either Kyle or Cole, one of his younger twin brothers.

A fat stream of water shot through the air, hitting Kovol squarely in the back. It knocked him off balance, and Elliot rolled out from under his foot.

Elliot sat up on his elbows. Kyle and Cole were nearby with a kinked hose they had somehow dragged all this way into the woods. Behind them were Wendy, Reed, Cami, and, for some reason, Tubs.

"What are you doing here?" Elliot asked

"I told them about you," Cami said. "I told them everything. Maybe you can't tell your secrets, but I can."

Elliot scrambled to his feet and ran over to them.

"King, huh?" Reed said, his mouth in a half smile. "How funny is that?"

"This isn't a joke," Elliot said. "You have to run away from here."

"And miss all this fun?" one of the twins said. They released another spurt of water at Kovol, knocking him back down.

"We came to help you fight," Wendy said. "When Mom and Dad are at work, they tell us to take care of each other. Well, that's what we're doing."

"They meant to be sure we all eat dinner and get our homework done," Elliot said. "Not help fight Underworld wars!"

"Yeah, yeah," Tubs said. "Duck."

Elliot ducked down, and Tubs lobbed a rock at Kovol, clonking him on the forehead and knocking him down again.

"Now's your chance," Cami said. "We got that ugly beast distracted. Now use some magic to finish him off."

"I'm not sure I have any magic left," Elliot said. "If I do, it'll take a while to charge up again." He took a deep breath. "Besides, we'll just be fighting him all day unless I can finish making that potion."

"I brought it," Cami said, holding up the bottle of turnip juice.

"Water!" the twins yelled and sprayed Kovol again, but this time he was ready. He used a shield to push the stream of water back onto Elliot's family. Kyle and Cole dropped the hose, and everyone scattered behind the nearest tree, bush, or rock where they could fit.

Elliot had chosen a thick bush off to the right. From there he saw Wendy and Reed behind nearby oak trees, dripping wet. The twins had squeezed together behind a large rock. Cami was in another bush. And...where was Tubs?

Elliot peeked out to where Tubs stood facing Kovol. In his hands was another rock.

Kovol looked confused. "You're not running," he said.

Tubs's eyes narrowed. "I know all about you, jerk. You're just another bully, a loser who tries to make himself feel better by hurting others. I know that, because I used to be a bully too."

"Nobody insults Kovol," the Demon said.

"I used to think nobody insulted me either," Tubs answered. "They do, but they say the insults behind your back. You should've heard what the kids used to say about me."

Elliot was pretty sure a lot of kids still said those things about Tubs. But it was true—ever since Elliot had stood up to Tubs, he didn't bully people anymore.

"I'm the most powerful creature in the world!" Kovol yelled.

Tubs snorted. "If you were powerful, you wouldn't have to be mean. Elliot's the nicest kid I know, and he's more powerful than you'll ever be!"

Kovol roared. Then Tubs threw the rock at him, which bounced off his chest like a rubber ball. Kovol widened his hands for some magic.

"No!" Elliot leapt from his hiding place and dove for Tubs to knock him out of the way. However, just as before when they had played Capture the Flag, Tubs wasn't going anywhere. He was a lot thicker than Elliot, so Elliot only crashed into the side of Tubs's body and landed on the ground.

Tubs grabbed Elliot's arm and yanked him to his feet, then said, "If I don't get to bully this dork, then nobody does!" Tubs's idea of friendship, Elliot figured.

"Everyone start throwing things," Elliot yelled. "Whatever you can find!"

From their hiding places, Elliot's family and Cami threw rocks, sticks, and whatever else they had. Wendy threw a tube of her favorite lipstick. Reed threw packages of pickle relish. Cami threw some coins from her pocket. At first Elliot wasn't sure what the twins were throwing, but then he recognized them as the burned chicken nuggets from Wendy's dinner last night. He didn't blame them. If his pants pockets weren't full of holes, he'd have hidden his dinner there too. He wondered whether Wendy would be happy or angry to learn that her dinner had just been turned into a weapon. Probably a little of both.

None of the items hurt Kovol, but they distracted him. He couldn't defend against everything, so he tried just zapping the items as they got close to him.

The distraction gave Elliot a chance to run behind Kovol. He might not have any magic yet for a fight, but when he did have magic earlier he had prepared something special for a moment just like this.

Once Elliot had gotten a good head start, he yelled at Kovol, "Tubs was right. You're nothing but a bully. I'm not afraid of you, and you'll never catch me."

Then he ran. If Elliot had learned anything from his days of being bullied, it was how to run away.

Still, Kovol was catching up to him fast, and the place Elliot wanted to get to was farther away than he remembered. But every plan has a point where there's no turning back. Elliot was way, way past that point.

Kovol started sending shots of magic forward, almost like lasers. They hit the trees beside Elliot, punching huge holes through their trunks. Elliot began running in a zigzag pattern so that Kovol wouldn't know where his target would be next.

The zigzag slowed Elliot down, and Kovol was still getting closer. If he hadn't been so interested in hitting Elliot with magic, he might have figured out that he could probably grab Elliot if he reached out far enough.

Just ahead was a patch of ground with a brown haze over it. Elliot headed directly for it. He recognized the carefully laid-out leaves where he had magically marked the place where he should jump. When he reached it, he leapt forward as far as he could.

Kovol clearly didn't know the leaves were a signal to jump. He continued running forward…straight into the gripping mud…again.

"There's no gripping mud on the surface world," Kovol said, thrashing at the mud.

Elliot stopped and turned back to him. "There is now." He raised his hand to see if he had any magic to use on Kovol, but still there was nothing. He didn't think Kovol had gotten all of his magic, but he'd taken a lot of it, and he needed time to build it up again. Time was the one thing Elliot didn't have. (Well, that, and a solid gold time machine, but he wasn't thinking about that just then.)

"I can still fight you from here," Kovol growled.

"Not if you can't see me," Elliot said, already running away. "Until then, you're stuck."

Chapter
25

Where the Juice Is Shaken or Stirred

Elliot left the mud pit and ran toward his brothers and sister, who were on their way to find him. Wendy grabbed him first and closed him into a hug almost as tightly as the way Kovol had squished him before.

"Okay, okay." Elliot pushed away until he could breathe. "I'm fine."

"Hey, Elliot," Kyle said. "Me and Cole were thinking that if you're the king of these cookies—"

"Brownies."

"Yeah, Brownies. If you're the king, then what can we be?"

Cole punched a fist into the air. "We want to be your royal knights of the round table."

"I don't have a round table," Elliot said. "And I don't have any knights."

"Still, this is pretty big news," Reed said. "I thought it was exciting when I got that promotion last month at the Quack Shack, but that wasn't nearly as cool as this."

"I'm sorry I didn't tell any of you," Elliot said. "I couldn't, or else the Brownies would have gone away forever. And they needed my help."

"That's forgiven," Wendy said. "But now that we know, we want to help you. Cami said you have magic."

Elliot shrugged. "Kovol pulled most of the magic out of me. The Brownies say that when they use their magic too much, they have to wait a while until it works again, sort of like recharging a battery. All I can hope is that I have enough magic left to charge up."

"Where's Kovol now?" Cami asked.

"Stuck in gripping mud." Elliot didn't have time to explain what gripping mud was, but his siblings didn't seem too curious. As long as Kovol was stuck, that seemed to be all they cared about.

"So send all of your Underworld friends to get him now," Reed said.

Elliot shook his head. "That won't work. Even stuck in

the mud, he's still powerful enough to put up a good fight. As soon as it's dark enough, he'll call his army to help him get out. They're called Shadow Men, and they're just as scary as they sound. I don't want to fight Kovol anymore until I know I can win. It's time to end this." He looked at Cami. "Where's Harold?"

"He's still afraid to make another mistake." Cami frowned. "He said if he does, then I might not like him back. I told him nobody cares when people make mistakes. They only care when people don't try to fix them."

"So is he coming?"

Cami shrugged. "He said he'll think about it."

"Oh, good grief," Elliot said with a sigh. "Where's the turnip juice?"

She handed it to him. "Here. But you said it isn't ready yet."

"It's not. And I really don't know how to get that last ingredient." Then he remembered that his sister's food sometimes tasted a little strange. "Hey, Wendy, you don't happen to cook with earwax, do you?"

She made a face. "Ha-ha."

"No, seriously. Last week you made some cookies. I kind of thought—"

"I don't cook with earwax!"

He held up a hand. "No, I didn't think so." At least a big part of him had hoped not.

"You need earwax?" Tubs stuck his finger in his ear and pulled out a slimy clump. "I've got some."

"Thanks, Tubs," Elliot said. "But I need a lot of it for this potion to work."

"How much do you need?" Tubs reached into his pocket and pulled out a plastic sandwich bag with a huge blob of earwax inside. It was every color of gross, and so large he must have been collecting it for years.

"Disgusting!" Cami said. "How long have you had that?"

"Since I started preschool," Tubs said. "Do you like it?"

"No!" Cami and Wendy said together.

"Yes!" Kyle and Cole said at the same time.

Reed said nothing. Either he didn't have a very strong opinion on the subject of earwax collections, or else he was too grossed out to speak.

Elliot held out his hand for the earwax. "Well, I love it. Can I have it?"

Tubs pulled it closer to himself. "I dunno. I almost threw it at Kovol before, when we were all throwing things, but then I remembered how long I've been working on this collection. I can't just give it away for nothing."

"How about to save the world?" Elliot said.

"Yeah, I guess that is pretty important." Tubs thought it over. "Will they print my name in the newspaper about what a hero I am?"

"Probably not. We'll never really be able to talk about what happened here."

Wendy stepped forward. "But I'll make you some of those cookies that Elliot says tasted like earwax. A whole plate of them. And maybe they'll be helpful in getting your head to make more earwax."

Tubs smiled as if that actually made sense to him. "Yeah, I'll save the world with this bag of earwax. And who knows? Maybe I can use the next glob to save the universe!"

Elliot didn't think earwax worked that way. But at least Tubs handed him the plastic bag.

Cami knelt on the ground and opened the bottle of turnip juice. Being careful not to touch any of it, Elliot pushed the earwax out of the bag and into the bottle. It plopped to the bottom in a big clump.

"Now stir that in with a stick!" Wendy said.

"Or just shake it up," Reed said. "That's how we mix things at the Quack Shack."

While Wendy and Reed argued about whether the drink should be shaken or stirred, Elliot put the lid on and held it under his arm. He didn't think either one mattered. Minthred hadn't mixed it up, so neither would he. Besides, if he got Kovol to drink it, it was all going down in one swallow anyway.

"How's your magic doing?" Cole asked. "Is it back yet?"

"I don't think so," Elliot said.

"It had better hurry," Kyle said. "It's getting dark."

Elliot had noticed the same thing. In the woods, the trees were taller and the leaves denser, so it always felt dark earlier here than it would in Sprite's Hollow. And it definitely was getting late. At least, Elliot had felt his hungry stomach rumbling for some time.

A cool wind washed over Elliot's face. As long as the breeze was cool, that was only the weather. But any moment now the wind would shift, coming from Kovol's direction. And it would feel warm, even hot. It would be a signal that the Shadow Men had come.

"What happens now?" Reed asked.

Elliot's original plan with the potion had required the use of magic. He didn't have that option now, and he really wasn't sure how to trick Kovol into drinking the potion.

"Tell him you have this yummy drink and he can't have any of it," Cami said. "People always want things more if they know they can't have it."

This wasn't always true. One day each month, the school cafeteria had Mystery Meat Day. All the kids were pretty sure that meant the lunch ladies took the leftover meat from every other meal that month and ground it all together. And each month, the principal got first in line for lunch, then told the students they couldn't have any because it was all for him. It was his way of getting the kids to hurry into the line with him. But it never worked. As far as the kids were concerned, the only mystery with that meal was how many of them would lose their lunch before the day ended.

Despite that, Cami's suggestion was pretty good. Except for Mystery Meat Day, an idea like that usually worked.

"I'll try it," Elliot said. "But I've got to hurry. I want Kovol to drink this before he calls his army. All of you, stay here."

Chapter 26

Where Kovol Gets Jealous

Elliot returned to the patch of gripping mud where Kovol was still stuck. With mud pulling at Kovol's arms, he still folded them and frowned at Elliot. Kovol said, "The only reason I'm not attacking you now is that it will be much more fun once I'm free."

"Yeah, whatever." Elliot held out the bottle of juice. "I don't care, because I just drank some of this…um…yummy stuff. And you can't have it."

"Why would I care about that drink?" Kovol asked. "I have a much better drink, and you can't have it either."

"Why not?" Elliot asked. "I want some!" If it was good enough for a super villain, it was good enough for him. Then his eyes widened. Kovol was only using Elliot's own trick against him. Rude!

So Elliot stuck out his chest and said, "My drink made me stronger than you. I could snap you in half with my two fingers."

Kovol rolled his eyes. "You couldn't snap a twig."

"Oh, yeah?" Elliot picked up a nearby twig to prove him wrong. But he must have grabbed a really strong one, maybe one made of metal or something, because it wouldn't snap, even when he used all of his fingers. With a sigh he dropped it on the ground and broke it with his foot. "Aha!"

Kovol yawned, then pointed at a nearby tree branch. It cracked in half and almost fell right on top of Elliot's head.

"Show-off," Elliot muttered. This wasn't going so well.

He tried a different idea. "I'm sorry I pulled out your hair. I never planned to make you go bald. But if you want my opinion, it looks better now than if you tried to comb over that one hair to fool people."

"I'm not doing this because of the hair," Kovol said. "I'm doing this because I'm evil."

"I've met other evil creatures in the Underworld," Elliot said. "You're the worst, of course, but from what I've seen, if you decide that you want to change and become good, you can do that."

Kovol smacked hard at the mud, sending the message that his current life plans had nothing to do with becoming good. He would never help old ladies cross the road (unless he could eat them on the other side), or plant flowers (except maybe a prickly cactus), or do anything that a good creature would.

"Maybe you should just sit there and think about it a while longer." Elliot eyed the bottle of turnip juice. "Do you want a drink while you wait?"

"The last time I had a drink like that I fell asleep for a thousand years," Kovol said. "The great wizard Minthred tricked me."

Elliot snorted. "Oh, yeah, you were tricked by the most powerful goat-herding wizard of all time, no doubt. All right. I'll be back in a while and see if you changed your mind about the drink." He started to leave, then froze. Something in the air had changed.

He looked up at the skies, but the dimming air suddenly became as black as midnight. It wasn't that late yet. Which meant only one thing. The Shadow Men were coming. There were so many of them overhead that they had blocked out any remaining light.

Kovol sent a charge of energy straight toward Elliot. It hit the bottle of turnip juice first, throwing it high into the air where it landed somewhere far away. The remaining energy crashed into Elliot's chest, and his body hit against a tree with a hard *oomph* before sliding back to the ground.

While Elliot lay there, breathless, the Shadow Men gathered around Kovol to pull him free of the gripping mud.

Since they were made of little but smoke and flame, it took all of them to lift Kovol's massive body. But when they stepped away, Kovol stood on solid ground, dripping with mud. And well rested to finish the fight.

Slowly, the entire army turned to face Elliot. Sweat from their intense heat rolled off his forehead. He had no magic to fight any one of them, much less this entire army. Yet he stood, prepared to give it his best try.

Then a small body poofed in front of him. "Stand back, Your Highness," Mr. Willimaker said. He held a long stick of bright light. "I'll protect you."

"So will I," Fudd said, appearing beside Mr. Willimaker. He wasn't facing in the correct direction, but his stick of light was held high and ready.

"You're both healed too?" Elliot said.

"Everyone in the cold comas has been healed," Fudd said. "They're only waiting in the Underworld long enough to get their light from Agatha. Then they'll come to help you too."

And sure enough, one by one more creatures poofed in. As they did, the Shadow Men backed farther and farther away. By now they knew what those sticks of light could do. And with each new creature who arrived, their chances got worse.

"Give the word and we'll attack," Mr. Willimaker said.

Elliot nodded and then called out, "Creatures of light, *we* are the strong ones, not them! Darkness can only exist where there is no light. And each of you holds in your hands the power to chase away the darkness forever. They can give you a burn, or suck warmth from your body, or even take your eyesight. But you are holding the power to destroy the darkness. We will not leave these woods until the curse is ended and Kovol remains alone. Creatures of light, attack!"

They rushed at the Shadow Men, swinging their sticks in every direction they could. With each hit, ashes fell to the ground like black snow. Kovol tried fighting in defense of his army, but everyone was moving too quickly, so he had no idea where to send his magic. From where Elliot stood, it was hard to see if anyone was winning, but so far his side definitely wasn't losing. Still, there were so many more on their side than his.

From the trees behind him, someone whispered, "Hey, this is cool. Good job, little brother."

"Reed!" Elliot hissed. "I told you to stay back."

"Yeah, we ignored that. You're the Brownie's king, not our king. So where can we get some of those sticks?"

"This is their fight," Elliot said, "but I need you to spread out and look for the bottle of turnip juice. Kovol threw it somewhere, but I don't know where or how far away."

"So your Brownies get the fun job," Reed said with a sigh. "All right, fine. We'll find that bottle."

Less than a minute after Reed left, Kovol must have had

enough of the battle, because he let out a roar loud enough to shake the tops of the trees. Everyone froze. Kovol charged forward and grabbed Elliot, lifting him high into the air. "Drop the sticks, or I'll eat your king right now."

Without a moment's hesitation, the sticks clattered to the ground.

And unexpectedly, Elliot laughed. "I know the real reason you stopped the fight," he said. "You are so jealous."

"What?"

"You're jealous because all these creatures came to fight the Shadow Men. Nobody wants to fight you."

"They can't fight me, because I'm so powerful." Kovol's voice was angry, but maybe a little worried too.

"There's only one of you, and there are hundreds of Shadow Men," Elliot said. "You're only as strong as the last thing you ate for dinner. You can't even escape gripping mud without them. But they're always strong. Stronger than you. Scarier than you. More powerful than you'll ever be."

"*I* am the most powerful!" Kovol boomed. "They are my army. I cursed them to life!"

"They're not alive, so they don't die," Elliot said. "But you could. That makes *them* the most powerful creatures in the Underworld."

"I will win this war," Kovol said. "Me, and only me! And nothing is as strong as Kovol!"

Elliot tried not to smile. "There's only one way for you to be as strong as them."

Kovol might not have fallen for the turnip juice trick, but he fell for this one perfectly. Forgetting about his plans for Elliot, Kovol turned toward his army. He blew out all the air from his lungs, then began sucking it back in, tugging at the Shadow Men with his breath, just as he had pulled magic from Elliot's body. One by one the Shadow Men were dragged into his mouth, swallowed up whole. Large rings of smoke blew out of his ears, and with each eaten Shadow Man, Kovol's body grew larger and darker. He filled himself with their flames and their powers to curse. If he was bad before, then he was horrible now.

"What have you done?" Mr. Willimaker whispered to Elliot.

"We could never have beaten his entire army," Elliot said. "Kovol just made a big mistake."

"But he has all of their power now," Mr. Willimaker said. "His entire army is within one body."

"And in *only* one body. Don't worry, my friend, the best is yet to come." Elliot knew how to finish this now. He had a plan.

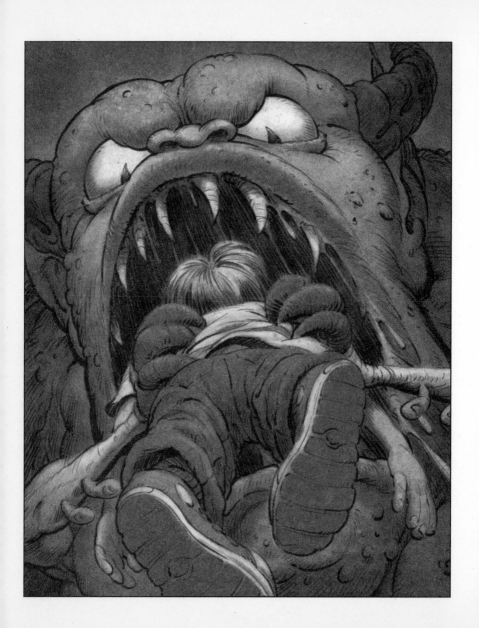

Chapter 27

Where Kovol Eats His Last Meal

Elliot ran out of the clearing and back into the woods. "Reed? Wendy? Where is everyone?"

"We can't find the bottle," Wendy said. She was with Kyle and Cole near a grove of tall trees, each of them searching as fast as they could.

"It's not over here!" Reed said with only his head poking out of a thick bush. Tubs was a little farther away, but he was still searching too, so Elliot knew neither of them had it.

"Where's Cami?" Elliot asked.

Reed pointed to his right, and Elliot went running in that direction.

"Cami?" he called.

"Over here!" she answered. "I think it's close. I can see the broken branches where it must have landed, but it rolled away somewhere."

Elliot walked toward Cami's voice until he found her, and together they followed a trail as wide as the bottle down a steep hill.

He spotted the bottle first. "There it is!" He started toward it, then something hit him in the back and he yelled in pain and fell forward.

"Elliot!" Cami screamed, running beside him.

"I'm all right," he said, holding his back. "One of Kovol's shots must've hit me."

"Are you really all right?"

"Yeah," he muttered. "It's just—that sort of hurt. A lot."

"Let me look at it."

"No way," Elliot said. "Girl germs."

"Oh, good grief. There's no such thing." Cami lifted up his shirt enough to look at his back. "Wow, I see some sort of mark there about as long as my thumb. Are you sure you're okay?"

The hit had knocked the breath out of him and stung a little at the time. He had no idea what kind of mark was on his back, but as far as he could tell, he was fine.

"Call one of your Brownies to come look at it," Cami said.

"Maybe later," he said. "Just get that bottle."

"I think I know your plan," Cami said. "I'll take care of it if you can get Kovol there."

From the top of the hill, Kovol yelled, "Show yourself, Elliot, so that I can destroy you!"

Elliot couldn't think of a better reason *not* to show himself. But he didn't want Kovol aiming that magical energy at any of his friends or family.

Elliot slowly stood, but a voice behind him called, "Okay, but which of us is Elliot?"

Elliot turned and behind him saw...himself. In Elliot's form, Harold stood in front of Cami, blocking her body with his.

Kovol sent more balls of energy down the hill, but he wasn't sure which Elliot to fight, so he wasn't aiming well. It was easier for Elliot to dodge his attacks this time, which was good because his back still stung and he was moving slowly.

As Harold blocked the balls, he declared, "Cami Wortson, you are the love of my life. Give me an order and I will obey."

"Puff us away from here!" she cried. "I've got the bottle. Puff us away."

Harold turned to her. "Uh, my love, the correct word is 'poof.'"

"Then poof us!" Cami screamed. "Hurry!"

"Ah, the love of my life nags with the sweetest voice," Harold said, although Elliot thought the expression on his face as they poofed away wasn't exactly the most loving.

Kovol roared when they disappeared, but Elliot stood, ready to face him. That hit on his back was exactly the jump-start his magic needed. He felt the energy of the Pixies again, pulsing and vibrating inside his body like a humming engine. But he didn't plan on using it. Not yet anyway.

"Are you the real Elliot or another fake one?" Kovol yelled.

"There's only one way to find out," Elliot said, already backing away. "You'll have to catch me and see for yourself."

Just as before, he ran and Kovol followed, his feet pounding into the earth behind Elliot like miniature earthquakes. Luckily, this was the very spot where he and Tubs and Cami had played Capture the Flag only that morning, and Elliot knew the area well. He only hoped Cami had done her part. He wouldn't have time to make sure, and there were no second chances.

"No more waiting," Kovol said. "When I see you, I will eat you."

"You'd better," Elliot said. "Because I'm the most powerful wizard since Minthred a thousand years ago. The only way to become as strong as me is to eat me."

"No!" Cole darted out from the bushes where they had been hiding. He ran up and kicked Kovol in the shin. "You can't eat our brother!"

"Hush!" Elliot hissed.

Then Kyle ran forward and said, "You won't even like him. Last year when Elliot and I were in a fight, I bit his finger and it tasted awful."

Kovol laughed, then picked up Kyle and tucked him under his arm. "I'll eat you next."

"No, you won't!" Elliot swerved around with the idea to do magic. He could play the trick he had used on Fidget before of "This is a stickup!" and Kyle would be free. The sticks would lift Kovol up in the air just as they had with Fidget. But he didn't know how much magic he had left or if it was strong enough to lift Kovol. There had to be another way.

Maybe he didn't need magic to trick Kovol. He remembered how he had gotten away from Tubs earlier that morning.

"Get me!" Elliot yelled. "Just me. But only if you catch me!" Then he ran back to Kovol, who dropped Kyle in his hope to grab on to Elliot. But Elliot crawled between Kovol's legs while yelling for his brother to run. Kovol leaned low to reach Elliot and then, just as Tubs had done, tumbled into a somersault. Elliot waited to be sure Kyle had gotten away, then circled around and continued his race.

The somersault only slowed Kovol for a moment before he was back on his feet running again. Elliot wasn't as far ahead as he would have wanted, but he hoped it was enough. Two steps before he reached the clearing where he and Cami had hidden their flag that morning, Elliot took a hard left turn and ducked behind a tree.

A moment later, Kovol came to the same clearing and stopped. If Elliot had wanted to hide, he was doing a terrible job. For there he was, just standing still, with no expression of worry or surprise on his face. In fact, all he had was some strange smile, as if he had a great secret.

"This is the end," Kovol said, charging forward for a final attack.

He picked up Elliot's body and crushed it like a soda can, then dropped the entire thing in his mouth.

And not two seconds later, the evil Demon fell flat on his face, sound asleep.

Chapter 28

Where Elliot Has a Scar

Cami was the first to jump from her hiding place after Kovol fell. Harold came out behind her, and she even gave him a quick kiss on his cheek, causing him to turn redder than a raspberry.

Kyle came out next and quickly got a punch in the arm from Cole, who had run after Kovol to save his twin brother.

Elliot was the last to step out from the tree. Just as he had known would happen, Kovol had eaten the paper-mache Elliot doll in one bite. Inside that doll was a very large jar of turnip juice, goat spit, and earwax.

And Kovol was sound asleep.

Mr. Willimaker and Fudd poofed in next. Mr. Willimaker gave Elliot the lowest bow he'd ever made, and when he explained to Fudd what had happened, Fudd also bowed to

Elliot. Then the other creatures who had fought the Shadow Men near the gripping mud appeared. They began cheering and dancing and singing.

Reed, Wendy, and Tubs ran in next. Wendy gave Elliot an enormous hug, and Reed patted him on the back. Tubs shoved his hands into his pockets and said, "That was pretty cool. Maybe you're not such a dork after all."

"We were so worried," Wendy said. "We saw Kovol hit you with that ball of energy and knock you over."

"It felt like he threw a bowling ball at me," Elliot said. "But other than a mark on my back, I don't think he did any damage."

"What mark?" Mr. Willimaker asked. "Let me see it."

Elliot turned and raised his shirt. "What does it look like?"

"It's a scar in the shape of a crown," Mr. Willimaker said. "Kovol tried to curse you, but whatever you were thinking about must have blocked the curse and saved your life."

"I was thinking that I didn't care what happened to me," Elliot said. "I only wanted to protect my family, and the Brownies, and the rest of the Underworld."

"That's a wizard's mark," Mr. Willimaker added. "Only the most powerful of all Underworld creatures ever get one of those."

"I'm no wizard." Then Elliot remembered that Minthred was only a goat herder. He probably never thought he deserved to be called a wizard either.

"Truly you have the heart of a king," Fudd said. "And today you saved us all."

Patches poofed in and immediately hugged Elliot's leg. "Elliot—I mean, Your Highness! I just heard the news! We'll throw a big party in Burrowsville to celebrate. We'll have everything yummy to eat there—carrot soup, cabbage pies, cauliflower cookies, all the best foods!"

"Yum," Elliot said. Even Wendy's scariest menu had never included cabbage pies.

"We'll have that party tomorrow night," Mr. Willimaker said. "Can't you see how tired the king is?"

"I am tired," Elliot agreed. "A party tomorrow would be better. Besides, we still have to figure out what to do with Kovol."

The Elf Slimy Toe Jam, or whatever his name was, stepped forward. "We have a plan for that, King Elliot. We shall create a home for him deep in the Underworld seas, where the Mermaids will keep watch over him. Even if another Shadow Man does exist, he'd never get through all that water to rescue Kovol. We feel that Kovol will sleep there forever."

Forever sounded pretty good to Elliot. He nodded his permission at the Elf, and then thanked him for Minthred's journal. "Maybe one day someone will write a book about my story too," Elliot said.

Mr. Tojam laughed. "A book about an eleven-year-old

human who becomes king of the Brownies and fights an Underworld war? Who'd ever believe it?"

Elliot joined in the laughter. "Yeah, that does sound pretty crazy. Thanks for taking Kovol to the Mermaids. And thanks again for letting me see Minthred's journal."

"You saved our world," Mr. Tojam said. "Thank you, King Elliot." He bowed, then snapped his fingers, and both he and Kovol disappeared.

"Until tomorrow night, then," Fudd said. "I'd offer to poof you home, but I know you still have Pixie magic, so you can probably get yourself there better."

"I could," Elliot said. "But for tonight I'll just walk home with my family. See you tomorrow." And that was the most ordinary thing Elliot had done all day.

Where Elliot Goes Home

Elliot remained pretty quiet for the rest of that night and through the next day. His parents got home sometime that morning, but nobody said anything to them about the Brownies or Kovol or the Underworld war. They had all promised Elliot they would keep his secret. And even though it wasn't much of a secret anymore, Elliot appreciated their promise.

It would take a long time for Sprite's Hollow to repair the many sinkholes throughout town, but at least there had been no new ones. All of the reporters got scientists to come on their news shows and explain that the sinkholes had been caused by a freak meteor storm several thousand light-years away. The scientists seemed to believe it, the reporters didn't seem to understand it, and everyone went on with their lives.

Elliot hadn't been the only one to notice that the sinkholes on Main Street were in the shape of his name. But then the mayor of Sprite's Hollow, Mayor George Fillat, convinced everyone that the sinkhole was in the shape of *his* name and said it was a sign that he should be reelected. His campaign slogan was immediately changed to "Protecting our town from all danger over and under the world!"

Elliot snorted when he heard that, but there wasn't much he could do about it.

That afternoon, Cami stopped by the house to check on Elliot. "You seem quiet," she said. "Everything okay?"

"Definitely," he said.

"I told Harold that I'm not the love of his life," Cami said. "I don't want to be the love of anyone's life right now, just their friend." She was quiet for a moment, then added, "Are we friends, Elliot?"

"Definitely." And in that moment, he didn't dislike her at all. Even calling her Toadface didn't seem so funny anymore.

"You want to play a game or something?" she asked. "And don't say definitely."

"Then I'll just say okay," he answered. They spent the rest of the afternoon in the backyard kicking a soccer ball around and then helping Cole and Kyle dig a hole for a new spring-time mud puddle.

When it was time for the party that evening, Elliot invited

his brothers and sister and Cami and Tubs to come along. The Elves would be in charge of poofing everyone down there, so he knew it would be a smooth ride.

The clearing in the center of Burrowsville was spread with tables and picnic blankets and food wherever it fit. Hundreds of creatures from every corner of the Underworld had come. Elliot recognized many of them as the creatures who had been turned to stone in Kovol's cave. With the Shadow Men gone, their curse had been lifted.

Standing near the front was Agatha, back into her usual Hag form. Elliot ran to her and wrapped his arms around her waist. "Thank you, Agatha," he said. "Nobody else but you could've healed everyone."

She patted his back. "And I knew no one but you could've saved the Underworld. Oh…oopsie."

Something wet and squishy plopped onto Elliot's head. Whatever it was, Agatha immediately picked it up and Elliot jumped back. Agatha had her hand pressed over her left eye.

"Eww!" he cried. "Did your eye just fall on my head?"

With a little pop, Agatha squeezed her eye back into place and laughed. "Don't be silly. Eyes don't just fall out." He reached up to check the top of his head for leftover eye parts, but she pushed his arm down. "I wouldn't do that. One moment, dear." She blinked, and he felt a breeze pass through his hair. "Yes, that's better now."

"What did—" Elliot stopped. "Never mind. I won't ask."

She smiled. "I am a Hag, and these words you must know. I'll always admire you, wherever you go."

Elliot grinned back at her. "Thanks, Agatha."

Mr. Willimaker ran up to Elliot. "Your Highness! Here's your crown!"

The crown was small enough that it would have fit better on Elliot's wrist than his head, but he put it on anyway. His family was given their choice of seats, and then Mr. Willimaker led Elliot up to his toadstool throne.

Fudd was already sitting beside Elliot's throne. He was facing backward and hopelessly trying to find his cup of Mushroom Surprise drink when Elliot sat down.

Gently, Elliot put a hand on Fudd's shoulder and steered him to the correct position. Then he handed Fudd his drink.

"Thank you, Your Highness," Fudd said.

Elliot picked up his own cup of Mushroom Surprise—his favorite of all Underworld foods—and clicked it against Fudd's cup. "Cheers!" he said.

"What should we toast to?" Fudd asked. "To a long reign for King Elliot, of course!"

"I think a better toast is a lifetime of happiness for all Underworld creatures," Elliot said.

"Yes, Your Highness." With that, Fudd pushed back his chair and stood. For once facing in the correct direction, he raised his cup to the crowd in front of him and said, "When Elliot was made our king, I was the last Brownie to cheer for him. So I want to be the first of all Underworld creatures to officially thank him for what he has done. In honor of Elliot Penster, king of the Brownies, may we toast to a lifetime of happiness for all creatures who helped bring peace to the Underworld. And a lifetime of happiness to the human, King Elliot, and his family and friends."

At once, the entire audience clicked their cups together and said, "To all, a lifetime of happiness."

With that, the dinner was served. Elliot ate very little of what was offered to him, in part because most of it wasn't food he really liked, but also because the only thing he really wanted to do was look over the crowd and try to memorize as many faces as he could.

When dinner was over, Mr. Willimaker nudged Elliot on the arm and asked, "Is there anything you want to say, Your Highness?"

There was. Elliot stood and the crowd went silent. "You've all said a lot of nice things about me ever since I became king," he began. "That's been really cool, but I think none of those things were true *until* I became the king. I was just an ordinary kid before. And the thing is, I'm still an ordinary kid. But I had to learn that even someone ordinary can do something extraordinary."

The creatures in the crowd looked at one another as if they wanted to clap for Elliot. But something in the way he spoke suggested he didn't want them to clap. He only wanted them to understand. So they nodded softly and waited for him to finish.

Elliot's smile widened. "When I first became king of the Brownies, they were ordinary too. But you all saw the way they fought yesterday. They might not have the strength of the Goblins, or the sneakiness of the Pixies, or the grace of the Elves. But you saw their bravery and loyalty in the fight against Kovol. They've learned to be extraordinary too." Then he looked down for a moment. "And because we both understand that, it's time for the Brownies to have a new king."

A gasp spread across the audience. Patches stood up from her seat and yelled out "No!" then ran up the aisle near him. When she got close, her father took her hand and held her back.

"You know it's time for this, and so do I." Elliot said it to everyone, but to his friends most of all. He would miss the Brownies and they would miss him, but they also deserved a ruler who could always be here in Burrowsville with them. And he was ready to just be Elliot Penster, ordinary eleven-year-old kid, again.

"What will we do without you?" Mr. Willimaker asked.

"You will be the chief royal advisor," Elliot said. "Any time the ruler of the Brownies needs help, you are the first person to talk to. No one gives better advice, and no one has served me with more loyalty."

"But what if the Brownies get into trouble again?" Patches asked. "There's no one as clever as you, Elliot."

"Sure there is. Patches, you are smarter than anyone else I've met down here. I want you to be the chief royal scholar. If there's anything the ruler needs to know, you are in charge of figuring it out."

Patches bowed low. "Yes, King Elliot."

"I'll serve the new ruler any way I can," Fudd said. "Though I know with my blindness, I won't be as much help as I want to be."

"Your blindness only helped us to see you better, how good and loyal and strong you are," Elliot said. "But it won't be a difficulty for you any longer."

Fudd shook his head. "There's only one way to heal this curse of the Shadow Men, and that's—"

"That's for a magical creature to give up his magic," Elliot said. "I still have a little of the Pixie magic left."

Fudd shook his head. "No, Your Highness. If you're ever in trouble on the surface world, that magic can save you."

"I'll never be in as much trouble as I've had down here," Elliot said. "I don't need the magic. Just my friends and family."

Tears streamed down Fudd's cheeks. "Don't do this for me, please. I'm not worth it."

Elliot put a hand on Fudd's shoulder. "You're my friend. Besides, I'm still the king. You don't get to tell me no. Patches, how do I do this?"

"Put your fingers over his eyes," she instructed.

Elliot knelt in front of Fudd and put his fingers over Fudd's eyes. The magical vibrations he had felt inside him rose from his chest and traveled out his fingers, and then they were gone.

As the magic entered his body, Fudd stumbled back and fell to the ground.

"Are you okay?" Mr. Willimaker asked.

Fudd rolled to his stomach, then pushed himself up. He put a chubby hand in front of his face and wiggled his fingers, then began laughing. "I see my hand! I can see!" He picked up a spoon and looked at himself in the reflection, "Argh! I forgot how ugly I am." He ran to Elliot, still laughing. "You are a great king, Elliot. Thank you, thank you for what you've done. But I'm sorry to take your magic."

"You didn't take it. I wanted to give it to you," Elliot said, "and to give you this too." He took the crown off his head and handed it to Fudd. "You are the king now."

Fudd shook his head. "Me? There are other Brownies who deserve it more."

"You don't become king because you deserve it. You become king because the Brownies deserve you." He raised his cup of Mushroom Surprise again. "Long live King Fudd."

The entire audience raised their cups. "Long live King Fudd," they all repeated.

Elliot smiled. "It's time for me to go home now." He walked down to his brothers and sister, let Reed punch him lightly on the arm, and then said, "We need someone to poof us there."

Several Elves stepped forward, but Fudd raised a hand. "It will be my honor to send Elliot on his last trip home from the Underworld."

"Just one minute," Elliot said. "Everyone move back." Thanks to the Mushroom Surprise, he burped out the king of all burps. Or at least the former king of all burps. It knocked over the nearest table and melted the tablecloth. "I have to admit, I will miss that," Elliot added. Then he stepped back. "Now it's time."

And with that, Elliot closed his eyes, felt the last tug in his gut, and opened his eyes back in his room. Reed sat on his bed across from Elliot.

"That was pretty cool," Reed said. "Are you okay?"

Elliot smiled. "Yeah. Everything is great."

And for the next day and the next and every day after, Elliot played and learned and laughed as any ordinary kid would. Every once in a while, though, he would stop when he smelled the very strong odor of pickles. And sometimes a pointy brown hat would peek out from behind a bush. And he would know that even though he was no longer the king, a part of him would always belong to the Brownies.

Warning: Any similarity between this story and any actual story of an eleven-year-old king of the Brownies fighting an Underworld war is, believe it or not, a really freaky coincidence. Seriously, what are the odds of that?

Acknowledgments

All my affection and appreciation to Jeff, who is my best friend, partner in crime, and love of my life. Warm thanks also to Ammi-Joan Paquette, who has been coach, counselor, therapist, friend, and agent extraordinaire. And to Kelly Barrales-Saylor, Kay Mitchell, and the many wonderful people at Sourcebooks who gave of their time and talents to build this series. My sincere thanks to you all.

Special thanks should also go to the Pixie Princess, Fidget Spitfly. Without her help to Elliot, the last Underworld War might have turned out very differently. Although to be fair, without Fidget there probably wouldn't have been an Underworld war in the first place. Then this book would have been called *Elliot and the Rather Uneventful Day*, in which Elliot wrestles with an ingrown toenail, and then has lunch.

About the Author

JENNIFER A. NIELSEN lives at the base of a very tall mountain in northern Utah with her husband, three children, and a dog that won't play fetch. Although she has never fought in any Underworld Wars, she did once engage in a battle to the death with a noisy cricket that had gotten loose in her house. The battle ended in a tie and the cricket is fine. We are less sure about the condition of the house.

About the Illustrator

GIDEON KENDALL graduated from the Cooper Union for Science and Art with a BFA and has since been working as an artist, illustrator, animation designer, and musician in Brooklyn.